"There are a lot of things you don't know about…"

"Really?" Max's eyes were unreadable. His muscles and his strong forearms rippled as he opened the bag of chips and then fished one out. "Want some?"

"No, thanks."

His boots were sprinkled with sawdust. His jeans were stained, but man, he looked so handsome.

"What are you afraid of, Hayley?"

His question about flattened her. "What?"

"You act like someone who is afraid. Guarded. You won't let me in. Who hurt you?"

You.

She tamped down the word and hopped to her feet. "I'm going to go see if my patient's here. Sometimes they come in early. Enjoy your lunch. I'll see you back at the house. Bye."

She rushed out of there before he could say another word. That had been so close.

Max was fun and flirty and made her feel like the only woman in the world—until a big, staggering mountain caught his eye and then he'd be gone.

There was no way she could endure losing him again.

Heidi McCahan is a Pacific Northwest girl at heart but now resides in North Carolina with her husband and three boys. When she isn't writing inspirational romance novels, Heidi can usually be found reading a book, enjoying a cup of coffee and avoiding the laundry pile. She's also a huge fan of dark chocolate and her adorable goldendoodle, Finn. She enjoys connecting with readers, so please visit her website, heidimccahan.com.

Books by Heidi McCahan

Love Inspired

Opportunity, Alaska

Her Alaskan Family
Lost Alaskan Memories

Home to Hearts Bay

An Alaskan Secret
The Twins' Alaskan Adventure
His Alaskan Redemption
Her Alaskan Companion
A Baby in Alaska

Love Inspired Trade

One Southern Summer
A Winter of Sweet Secrets

Visit the Author Profile page at LoveInspired.com for more titles.

LOST ALASKAN MEMORIES

HEIDI McCAHAN

If you purchased this book without a cover you should be aware that this book is stolen property. It was reported as "unsold and destroyed" to the publisher, and neither the author nor the publisher has received any payment for this "stripped book."

ISBN-13: 978-1-335-23024-9

Lost Alaskan Memories

Copyright © 2025 by Heidi Blankenship

All rights reserved. No part of this book may be used or reproduced in any manner whatsoever without written permission.

Without limiting the author's and publisher's exclusive rights, any unauthorized use of this publication to train generative artificial intelligence (AI) technologies is expressly prohibited.

This is a work of fiction. Names, characters, places and incidents are either the product of the author's imagination or are used fictitiously. Any resemblance to actual persons, living or dead, businesses, companies, events or locales is entirely coincidental.

For questions and comments about the quality of this book, please contact us at CustomerService@Harlequin.com.

® is a trademark of Harlequin Enterprises ULC.

Love Inspired
22 Adelaide St. West, 41st Floor
Toronto, Ontario M5H 4E3, Canada
www.LoveInspired.com

Printed in U.S.A.

He healeth the broken in heart,
and bindeth up their wounds.
—*Psalm* 147:3

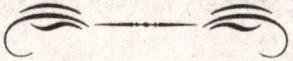

To my dear friends Lisa, Wendy and Linda Jo.
Thank you for our Monday and Friday morning
meetings. Your prayers, encouragement and
laughter have made me a better writer
and a better person. I am forever grateful.

Chapter One

How could one tiny human cry so much?

Hayley Morgan swaddled Fiona in a pink-and-white-striped blanket, then tucked the distraught infant in her arms and took another lap around the Butler family's spacious downstairs.

"I updated the shared spreadsheet so you'll know when she ate and had her diaper changed," Juliet said with a yawn, then slid a paperback romance novel into her purse. "There are two bottles of formula already mixed in the fridge."

"Got it. Thanks," Hayley said. "Go on. You deserve a long nap."

"Facts. She woke up four times last night." Jangling her car keys, Juliet walked toward the door. Her long, strawberry blond ponytail bobbed in time with her steps. "Text me if you need anything."

"I won't need anything," Hayley called after her as Juliet stepped outside. "Get some sleep."

Doubt swept in before Juliet backed her car out of the driveway. Hayley adored babies. She'd looked after Juliet when they were kids and their older brother had been so sick. When she was a teenager, she babysat the neighbors' kids quite a bit, and now that their older sister, Savannah, had a family, Hayley adored hanging out with her niece and nephew. But the thought of spending an entire Saturday alone with a three-month-old who rarely seemed content made her question her decision to accept this job. The pay was excellent, though and every dollar saved brought her a tiny bit closer to her dream of building an indoor recreation facility.

Wincing at the pitiful wails doing a number on her tender heart, Hayley tried quietly singing a popular country song.

Fiona cried louder.

"Okay, then. Not a fan. I get it. Your brother never liked my singing, either." Hayley paused beside the kitchen island, which was almost as big as the bedroom she used to share with her sisters, and grabbed a clean pacifier from the drying rack.

But Fiona twisted away when Hayley offered the pacifier, then worked her little fist free from the swaddle.

Hayley sighed. "Let's take another lap, sweet pea."

She left the kitchen, crossed the hardwood floor and stepped onto the plush beige carpeting in the family room. Buttery leather sofas formed an L-shape in front of a massive television mounted above an impressive fireplace. The well-appointed room, with its rustic beams overhead and wall-to-wall windows, granted her a breathtaking view of Opportunity, Alaska, the rugged small town she'd called home for most of her twenty-five years. She'd considered moving away after Max Butler had disappeared. Weston, the guy she'd dated when she'd been in school in Anchorage, had been so fun. She'd thought they might be headed toward a serious commitment. Until he'd found a job in California. But then she'd been hired as a physical therapy assistant at the clinic in Opportunity, and he hadn't been willing to give up his plans of living with his friends a few blocks from the beach. She couldn't blame him for wanting to be that close to the ocean. Honestly, though, she'd secretly hoped he'd move for her. Choose her. Because Opportunity was her home.

Besides, everyone she loved—except for Max—lived here.

Pushing aside thoughts of Max, Hayley drew a deep breath and focused on the infant in her arms. Fiona's thick shock of glossy dark brown hair swooped over her petite forehead. The baby's smooth brow wrinkled. Her eyelids fluttered, and she slurped on her chunky fist. Hayley moved closer to the windows and began swaying.

Outside, remnants of the recent snowstorm still dotted the yard as it sloped down the hillside toward Opportunity nestled beside the confluence of three rivers. In the distance, thick, billowy clouds cloaked Denali, the morning sun reflecting off its brilliant white facets.

"Now would be a great time for a nap, kiddo," Hayley whispered, gently stroking her finger down Fiona's nose.

Helping people filled her with satisfaction. Showing up and saving the day made her feel indispensable. Although she'd never brag about her innate talents—at least not where her sisters could hear her—sometimes she recognized a need even before the person knew they needed her.

It was like her own special superpower.

Fiona startled, then resumed crying, her perfect little fingertips clutching the edge of her blanket.

"Oh, dear. Maybe you're hungry?"

Good thing she hadn't bragged to anyone about meeting Fiona's needs, because she was struggling to keep the baby girl content. The poor thing cried more than anyone Hayley had ever babysat.

"I'd probably cry a lot too if I'd been separated from my parents," Hayley said softly. Jack Butler, Fiona's father, had offered Juliet and Hayley a ridiculous amount to babysit Fiona for six weeks. His young wife, Rachel, was at an inpatient treatment facility in California for postpartum depression, while Jack worked as a pilot for a large commercial airline, which often kept him away from home. He'd come back once in the ten days since Hayley and Juliet had taken on Fiona's care. But he had spent less than forty-eight hours at the house and all of twenty minutes holding Fiona before handing her off to Juliet, then leaving on his next trip to Paris.

"Let's go get your bottle ready." Hayley turned from the window. Fiona wailed louder. Unable to resist, Hayley snuck a glance at the photo of Max in a silver frame displayed on the metal-and-glass console table behind the sofa. He stood alone, grinning from the mountain's summit beneath a perfectly clear bluebird sky. He wore reflective sunglasses, his cheeks sunburned, his hands thrust in the air as if proudly declaring "achievement unlocked." That wide grin knifed at her insides. She reached over and put the photo frame face down. How she missed him. It had been two years since Max had left to summit a mountain in Peru. Two years since he'd gone missing. After a desperate search turned up nothing, eventually Max was presumed dead. His family had held a memorial service and grieved for his passing, but she hadn't been able to get over him. Not completely. A guy like Max left a gaping hole.

Fiona's angry cry pulled Hayley back to reality. "Come on, pumpkin. We'll get you fed. Maybe that will help cheer you up."

Hayley carried her into the kitchen. The baby girl's hair clung to her scalp, damp with sweat. "You miss your mama, don't you?"

If Fiona didn't settle down, Hayley might have

to call in reinforcements. Despite her pledge to Juliet that she wouldn't need anything. Their older sister Savannah and their mother had both offered to help if she got too overwhelmed. She'd already put in forty hours at the physical therapy clinic, so she might have to take Mom up on her kind offer.

As she warmed one of the bottles of formula Juliet had prepped, Hayley envisioned her bank account balance increasing after she deposited her half of the funds from Max's father. Every little bit helped. Between buying the property and funding the project, she needed over a million dollars, a hefty price tag for sure. And most days, the expense made her question if her plans were even worth the hassle. But she wasn't giving up.

But now, ten days in, exhaustion tugged at their frayed nerves. At least Mr. Butler had assured them that he'd come home next week to spend some time with Fiona after his trip overseas. She and Juliet were both looking forward to getting a break.

Why had she thought that being in Max's father's house and caring for his half sister would be easy? Wouldn't somehow reopen all of her old wounds? The night before Max had left for Peru, sitting around the firepit in her family's backyard, she had mustered the courage to tell him the truth. She'd admitted she'd fallen hard for him and dreamed of a future together. Maybe even marriage and a business partnership running the recreational venue. A solid team. But instead of choosing her, he'd wrecked her world when he told her his father's affair and the catastrophic demise of his family had left him cynical. Jaded.

I'm not husband material, Hayley, and I don't want to be a father, he'd told her, his deep voice laced with anguish. *Find yourself a man who still believes in happily-ever-after.*

He'd crushed her. And then he'd gone and disappeared. What was a girl supposed to do with a lousy ending like that?

Hayley returned to the living room and sat on the sofa. She settled Fiona in the crook of her arm and fed her the bottle. After drinking less than two ounces, Fiona's eyes closed and her mouth hung open. Her chest rose and fell in rhythmic breaths.

Thank You, Lord.

Hayley offered a silent prayer of relief. Then she slowly leaned forward and set the bottle on the coffee table. Juliet had suggested they figure out how to teach the baby to sleep someplace other than a human's arms. But she couldn't set Fiona down in her bassinet only to have her start crying again. Not now. The poor thing needed a good nap. Besides, Hayley had given her word that she'd help, and she was nothing if not devoted to meeting the needs of others. Even if it meant casting aside her own preferences.

As Fiona slept in her arms, Hayley's mind wandered back to Max and the way he'd looked at her with those intense blue eyes, full of pain and longing, before he'd disappeared from her life. How could she have been so blind to think that she could change his mind? That he would see sharing a life with her as more appealing than climbing a mountain? The pain of losing him still stung. She longed for the day when she'd meet someone who'd care for her. Love her. Help repair her shattered heart and fill the void that Max had left behind.

So this was home.

Max Butler stepped from the train Saturday afternoon, wincing as his swollen ankle protested. He limped toward a middle-aged man wearing a blue-and-white uniform and a faded ball cap. His face reddened with exertion as he stacked luggage on the platform.

Max briefly surveyed his surroundings. Patches of old snow dotted the parking lot. Birds chirped. The sun hid behind a bank of gray clouds. He shivered. His hoodie wasn't enough of a barrier against the frigid air enveloping him. Opportunity was much colder than the humid climate he'd left behind in Peru. People moved past him, some with phones pressed to their ears, and a car horn honked nearby. An older man embraced a young child, who giggled with delight as the man swooped him up in a circle. Max looked away, searching for something, anything familiar.

Not a single pang of recognition. No warm fuzzy feelings. And no one stepped forward to greet him. But that was what he'd wanted. Right? To come back on his own terms?

The attendant caught his eye. "Your bags are here, sir. Can I help you find a ride?"

"No, thanks." Max offered a tight smile. "I'll walk."

When Max reached for his faded green duffel bag, bulging at the seams, the man's concerned gaze traveled to Max's ankle. "Couldn't help but notice you're limping. Are you sure I can't arrange a ride? Folks are good about helping each other out around here."

Before Max could object, the man turned, cupped his hands around his mouth and hollered to a young guy standing nearby, chatting with another passenger.

The attendant turned back and gave Max a kind smile. "I'm sure Matthew will help. Do you have someplace in town you're planning to go?"

Max hesitated. He had the address of his family's house scribbled on a scrap of paper in his pocket. The thought of heading there made his palms sweat though. "Maybe to buy an ankle brace?"

"Good idea." He motioned for the younger guy to come closer.

"What's up?" Matthew asked, jogging over.

"When you have a minute, do me a favor and give my friend here a ride over to Carter's Sporting Goods."

"Sure thing." Matthew grinned and held out his hand. "What's your name?"

He shook the guy's hand. "Max."

"Nice to meet you." Matthew gestured to the luggage. "Any of this yours? I'd be glad to carry a bag or two. My truck's right over there."

Max followed where he pointed. A white Ford pickup truck sat by the curb.

"Thanks. That would be great. The green duffel is mine." Max fumbled in his pocket for a five-dollar bill, then offered it to the attendant who'd connected him with Matthew. "Appreciate your help, man. What'd you say your name was?"

He straightened, hesitated, then accepted the folded bill. "Pete."

"Thanks, Pete."

Pete smiled and tipped his cap. "Not a problem. Hope you find what you're looking for."

You have no idea. Max turned and followed Matthew toward his vehicle. Was he supposed to lead with his amnesia story each time he met someone? Or go with traumatic brain injury then left for dead on the side of a mountain in a foreign country? It was unbelievable, really, what had happened. He'd boldly shared a quick rundown of the facts with his seatmate on his long flight from Lima to Miami.

The woman had laughed and teased him about making up the story to flirt with her, but Max had been completely honest and not a little terrified about the journey. Not that he wanted to stay in Peru permanently, especially after the people at the US Embassy helped him reclaim his identity and secure a new passport. But his lack of memory prevented him from piecing together any details about his life before the accident. All he knew was that he was Max Butler, and he used to live in this town.

He discreetly glanced at the faces of the people they passed. Not that he'd recognize anyone because he had zero memory of any time he'd ever spent here.

Matthew opened the doors of his truck's extended cab, then slid Max's bag behind the front seat. "Where are you from?"

Max palmed the back of his neck. "This used to be home."

"Really? Have you been gone a while?"

Max nodded.

Matthew slammed the door. "You here for work or visiting family and friends?"

"Both."

It was true, he did want to see his family, reconnect with them. Except he didn't remember them and wasn't sure who was even in his family.

He climbed into the passenger side of Matthew's truck, sat and buckled his seat belt.

Matthew got behind the wheel. "How'd you hurt your foot?"

"Running to catch my flight. I had a tight connection in Dallas, but I stopped to help this lady whose kid had climbed out of his stroller. He took off running, and I went after him. Except I slipped in some water on the linoleum and turned my ankle."

"Wow." Matthew pressed a button to start the truck's engine. "No good deed, am I right?"

Max stared at him. Casual phrases, universal sayings that people seemed to intuitively understand, he was slow to pick up on. Frankly, it exhausted him, trying to pick apart the meaning of the words. "Are you the local taxi service?"

"Nah, I'm a courier." Matthew eased away from the curb and crossed the railroad depot's parking lot. "Package deliveries, that sort of thing. Pete probably figured I was headed in the same direction as you, so he asked me to help. It's a small town. We try to look out for each other."

Max nodded, drumming his fingers on his thigh as they left the parking lot. Matthew accelerated and Max took in the scenery. As they approached the center of Opportunity, his chest tightened. The building with the animal antlers mounted over the door came into view. That was it. A photo on the internet of that store had helped solve the mystery of his identity.

He twisted in his seat as the building flashed by.

"Everything okay?" Matthew tapped the brakes. "Need me to stop there?"

Max shook his head. "No. Just looking at the antlers."

"That place is legendary. I've seen more people take a selfie there than almost any place else in town."

"Cool." Max dragged his hand across his face. All the sensory input exhausted his weary brain. Once he'd bought an ankle brace and a few necessities, he'd have to find somewhere to crash and catch up on his sleep.

Matthew slowed at the caution light blinking over an intersection. Sunlight reflected off the nearby bridge spanning a river. When Matthew turned left, a massive mountain filled Max's vision, rising up from the tundra.

"Wow," he whispered.

"Yeah, even partially covered with clouds, Denali is really something, isn't it?" Matthew grinned at him. "Takes my breath away every time."

Max leaned forward to get a better view through the windshield. He'd always been a climber—that much he knew—and catching a glimpse of Denali sent a delicious thrill zinging through his veins. "I'd love to summit that mountain."

Matthew whistled low. "That's a bold move. Have you ever tried?"

Had he? Maybe. Yet another item on the long list of things he couldn't recall. Max settled back in his seat and went for a simple answer. "Nope. Have you?"

"No. I'm afraid of heights."

"Have you lived here long?"

"I moved here after college two years ago. It's a great little town to raise a family, but my girlfriend and I aren't ready to get married yet. You married?"

An inexplicable hollow ache caught his attention. Something skirted along the edges of his memory. He had loved somebody once, but he couldn't come up with a name, let alone a face.

Max shook his head, then turned and looked out the window. A rivulet of sweat tracked down his spine. Did he have a wife waiting here? What about kids? Hardly seemed likely. If he were someone's father, wouldn't his brain have at least remembered that? The physician in the village where he'd stayed had instructed him to be prepared for anything, though.

As if that were possible. How could he be prepared to greet the unknown? Maybe that explained the sweat dampening his skin.

"Here we are." Matthew tapped his blinker, slowed, and then drove into a parking lot.

"'Carter's Sporting Goods.'" Max read the sign mounted on the storefront aloud.

"Levi Carter and his dad run the store. Great people. If you need anything or have any questions, I'm sure they'd be glad to help you out." Matthew parked in a spot near the front door. "You want me to wait? You need a ride somewhere or—"

"No, I'm going to be a little while." Max unbuckled the seat belt and climbed out. "What do I owe you?"

"Nothing, man. Just pay it forward, all right?"

"Thanks. I'll see you around." Max got out, gingerly putting weight on his ankle. The swelling had gotten worse. His shoe felt like it was full of concrete. He shouldered his bag, then headed for the store entrance. A bell jingled as he stepped inside. The smell of leather and new shoes mingled with chocolate wafting from a container sitting on a table inside the door. He scanned the instruction card next to it. *Guess the wrapped chocolates in the plastic bin and enter to win a prize.*

He bypassed the table and limped forward, surveying the aisles nearby.

"Can I help you, sir?"

Max turned toward the man's voice.

"Oh, my. Max Butler?" All the color drained from his face.

"Yeah, that's me." Max smiled. Finally. Someone who knew him. He studied the guy's brown hair, kind eyes and shocked expression. Nothing seemed familiar. "I'm sorry, have we met?"

The man closed his mouth. Then opened it again. "Yeah, we've met. I'm Levi Carter. This is my family's store, and you used to be one of our best customers. Until you fell off the map."

"Yeah, about that." Max lowered his bag to the floor. "I can explain, but it's kind of a long story."

Hayley double-checked the buckles on the infant swing and made sure Fiona was secure in the cushioned seat, then slowly backed away. Fiona scrunched her pert little nose, hinting at her displeasure.

"Come on, cutie pie. You can do this," Hayley whispered. They'd spent almost ninety minutes on the couch this morning. Fiona had slept in her arms and Hayley had mindlessly watched HGTV, afraid to move. But now that she'd fed and changed the baby, she craved a few minutes to regroup. And update Juliet's spreadsheet.

She reached down and adjusted the soft music playing from the swing, then pressed the button to initiate the fancy contraption's gentle swaying motion. There. Fiona sighed as if she could barely tolerate the inconvenience of being separated from a human. Then she discovered the stuffed elephants and monkeys dangling above her head. She tucked her adorable little fist under her chin and stared at the animals orbiting on the swing's mobile.

"Stuffed critters for the win." Hayley smiled and then took a few more steps toward the kitchen. She only had three diapers left. A sad reality she and Juliet had somehow overlooked. Thankfully, their mom had responded to her desperate plea of a text and had promised to come by with diapers and lunch. Maybe she could persuade Mom to stick around and hold Fiona so she could get a quick workout in. The Butlers had an impressive home gym in the basement. A thirty-minute ride on the stationary bike or a run on the treadmill always boosted her mood.

She quickly tidied up the living area, taking her empty coffee mug and her plate from her morning snack to the kitchen. Muffled footsteps on the porch made her pause. Then someone knocked. She left her dishes in the sink and hurried toward the entryway.

She unlocked the dead bolt and opened the front door. "Hey, Mom, I hope you brought…diapers."

It wasn't her mom but her brother-in law, Levi, on the porch. Behind him, another man climbed the steps slowly, a faded green duffel bag slung over his shoulder.

Wait. He looked like— No. It couldn't be. Her stomach plummeted and she clawed at the doorframe, clutching the wood to steady her wobbly legs. "Max?"

His name sounded strangled as it left her lips.

"Yeah, he's, um…alive." Levi offered an empathetic smile. "Is it all right if we come in? You look like you need to sit down."

She pressed her palms to her cheeks. *Max*. Hot tears pricked her eyes. *How can this be?*

Max Butler stopped on the top step, his piercing blue eyes meeting hers. She surveyed his face. An appealing blond scruff marched along his angular jawline. He had the same ruddy cheeks, although he was a little bit gaunt. He looked exhausted. But the slope of his broad shoulders, that slight crook in the bridge of his nose, and the way he carried himself—confident. Strong. Determined.

That was all Max.

Her Max.

"Hayley?" Levi reached out and gently squeezed her forearm. "Can we come in?"

She couldn't move. Couldn't think. She could barely breathe. Somehow she forced her legs into motion and stepped back, pulling the door open. "You're alive," she said, unable to take her eyes off him.

An amused smile tipped up one side of his mouth. "That's what people keep telling me."

Levi stepped past her and went inside. Max moved closer. Her pulse sped. Would he hug her? He paused in the doorway, his imposing athletic body taking up more than its fair share of space. Her fingers itched to reach out and touch him.

But then he followed Levi without saying a word. That's it? No hug, no shoulder squeeze, nothing? Irritation knifed at her as she closed the door then faced them.

An awkward silence hung in the air. Max's bewildered gaze bounced between her and Levi. "Do I know her?"

What? Irritation morphed into anger. She wrapped her arms around herself. "That's not funny, Max. Of course we know—"

Levi held up his hand. "Hayley, Max sustained a traumatic brain injury. I'll let him share the details, but he has no memory of his life before his accident."

No way. She shoved her hands in the front pocket of her hooded sweatshirt to hide the trembling. "No memories at all?"

Max pinned her with a long look. "It's called retrograde amnesia. I can retain new information and create new memories, but I haven't been able to recall anything from before I fell."

Oh my. She swallowed against the tightness in her throat. She'd learned about traumatic brain injuries and memory loss in her training, but she'd never treated a patient with memory loss associated with head trauma. "That sounds awful. I-I'm so sorry."

"He's really been through it." Levi's concerned expression softened. "Max, does any of this look familiar?"

Max shook his head. "You said my father lives here?"

"With his wife, Rachel. But they're out of town," Hayley told him. "It's complicated."

If Max didn't know her and had no memory of his life in Opportunity, then he didn't know his parents, or their sordid history and contentious divorce. Or the plans she and Max had forged together. Was it up to her and Levi to tell Max everything he'd missed?

"Perhaps Hayley can bring you up to speed," Levi said. "I need to get back to the store."

Oh no.

Levi headed for the door, then turned back. "You mentioned diapers. I could get Savannah to bring some by. I'm sure we still have newborn sizes."

"I'm down to three, but Mom's on her way. If she doesn't get here soon, then I'll text Savannah."

Levi nodded, but he still didn't leave. "Are you sure you're going to be okay?"

"I'm in shock." She forced a smile. "But don't worry. We'll figure this out."

Levi had been married to her older sister Savannah for three years, and she'd known him her whole life. She'd never been great at concealing her true feelings. Was her panic over being alone with Max that obvious?

"I'll text you later, or else I'll ask Savannah to check in." He glanced over his shoulder. "We're glad you're home, Max."

Max turned from where he'd been examining a

framed picture of his father and Rachel. "Thanks, Levi. Appreciate your help."

Levi left, and Hayley closed the door, then faced the man she'd once offered her heart to, only to have him panic and reject her. He'd chosen a dangerous expedition in Peru instead of a relationship with her. Except he didn't remember, which meant she had no business bringing it all up. At least not now. Not here.

She shook her head. Never in her wildest dreams did she imagine Max would somehow be declared alive.

Max gestured to the photo. "Is this my father?"

Hayley nodded.

"But she's not my mother." Max frowned. "Too young."

Oh, wow. Her heart pinched. He really didn't know. "That's Rachel, your step, uh, your dad's current wife. Your mom lives in Montana now. I can help you call her or send an email or...whatever."

Max gave a brief nod and then reached for the photo frame she'd tipped over earlier. Uh-oh. She winced.

He righted it, paused, then held it out to her. "This is me. Which mountain is that?"

"Rainier. In Washington."

Nodding, he returned the frame to its proper place. "Any particular reason why it was tipped over?"

Because I missed you so much it hurts to see your face. I've never been able to get over you.

She couldn't bring herself to lead with the truth. "Must've knocked it over when I was cleaning."

Max's eyebrows knit together. "Do you live here?"

"Sort of."

His gaze slid to the swing. "That's your baby?"

"No, I'm not married. No kids, either. But your dad and Rachel have a newborn. Fiona. I'm taking care of her right now."

Frowning he scrubbed his palm across his face. "Okay, that's a lot to process."

"I can only imagine. Why don't you come into the kitchen? My mom should be here soon with lunch." She gently slid his duffel bag out of the way so her mom wouldn't trip when she came inside, then followed Max into the kitchen.

He stopped beside the island, his hands tucked in the pockets of his khaki cargo pants. "Nice place."

"Your dad and Rachel have a lovely home." She retrieved three glasses from the cabinet beside the sink. "Would you like some water? We have soda, lemonade and iced tea as well."

"Water's great. Thanks." His eyes followed her movements. "You said my dad is out of town?"

She filled the glasses with ice and water from the refrigerator's dispenser. "Yes."

"Without the baby?"

"Rachel isn't well. She's in California getting some medical attention, and your dad's a pilot. He's out of the country at the moment."

"And you're the nanny?"

"Yes, you could say that." She handed him his water, careful not to allow their fingers to brush. "My sister Juliet and I are caring for Fiona while her parents are away."

He hesitated, the glass halfway to his lips. "That's generous."

"Your dad pays well. Juliet has a student loan to pay off and she's trying to start her own business. I'm saving to build a...never mind. That's probably more than you needed or wanted to know."

Her cheeks flushed. Again. Why remind him that he'd walked away not only from a future with her, but their shared dream of opening an indoor recreation center?

"Details are important." Max smiled and her stupid, predictable pulse kicked up a notch, just like it always had when he smiled at her that way.

"Welcome home, Max. This town has missed you."

"Thanks. Guess I have a lot to catch up on."

"Guess so." Hayley avoided his eyes as she busied herself with wiping the already spotless countertop. Where was her mother?

"So Fiona is...my half sister?"

She nodded, then took a long sip of her water. Max's eyes softened as he watched Fiona in the swing. "I never imagined I'd have a sibling. It's... surprising."

Oh, boy. Fiona's existence was the least surprising detail about Max's former life. She racked her brain for something benign to say. "Your family will be so relieved to see you, especially after everything that's happened."

Once they got over their initial shock.

Max's expression darkened for a moment before he forced a smile. "Yeah, it's good to be back. Even if I have no memory of why I left in the first place."

Ouch. She set her water down, then quickly turned away and pretended she needed another paper towel from the dispenser beside the sink. How had he forgotten everything? And how would she even begin to tell him the truth? It felt cruel to reveal all the sordid drama between him and his family. Selfishly, she hated the thought of dredging up her heartache. Because she hadn't been enough for him. He'd told her to find someone else to love because he wasn't husband material. But it sort of felt like all he wanted was adrenaline-fueled expeditions. Rather than building a life with her. Now she suspected by the way he studied that picture of himself on Mount Rainier that adventure was still in him. And she wanted nothing to do with a man she couldn't rely on.

Chapter Two

He had a family.

Max glanced over his shoulder at the baby in the fancy swing. He couldn't stop looking at her. An unexpected wave of emotion tightened his throat. He swallowed hard, determined to keep it concealed from the perky woman with the gorgeous auburn hair standing on the other side of the kitchen counter. His arrival had obviously shocked her. If she caught him tearing up over a baby, she might suggest he move on.

And he couldn't afford that. He hadn't learned much about Opportunity, but he didn't have a job lined up. So this huge house was his best option for a place to stay while he got his bearings.

If he could figure out how to ask Hayley.

She kept busy, stepping around him and setting the table in the corner by the window. "Do you have people over for lunch often?"

"Only when I'm running low on diapers." Hayley flashed him a sheepish smile. "Just kidding. To be honest, Fiona loves to be held, so if there's an extra set of hands nearby, it makes mealtimes a little easier for everyone."

"I can hold her. I helped with kids all the time in Peru."

The silverware clattered to the table. Fiona cried out.

Uh-oh. He winced. "Did I say something wrong?"

Hayley hesitated, her mouth quirked to one side. "No. It wasn't wrong. I'm just…remembering how much you liked hanging out with kids when you lived here. I'm not at all surprised that's who you gravitated toward in Peru. Is that where you've been all this time?"

He nodded. "I didn't have any idea who I was when I woke up after my head injury. That was terrifying. Unfortunately, the two guys I'd been climbing with didn't survive, so I had no other option except to rely on the kindness of strangers. There were people who took care of me and helped with my recovery. When I was able, they put me to work."

Her eyebrows sailed upward. "What kind of work?"

"Played with the kids, helped carry water from the well, and did some odd jobs here and there."

"So how did you figure out that you're Max Butler and this is your hometown?"

His ankle was killing him. He had to sit down. "Funny story. A tourist had a picture on her phone of that store in town, the one with the antlers."

"Really? The General Store?"

Max claimed a seat near the window. "That picture sparked something in my mind. A vague memory that made me wonder if I'd been there before. And she was kind enough to tell me the store was in Opportunity, Alaska. So after a lot of paperwork, and about a dozen email messages, someone at the US Embassy helped me get a new passport."

Hayley paused and glanced at Fiona, who thankfully had settled down. "Did you lose all of that in your accident?"

"Very few of my personal possessions were recovered. A sleeping bag, two shirts and some climbing gear turned up, but that's about it. My ID and climbing permit have never been found. The only way the rescue team identified me was because I'd written my name on my sleeping bag with a permanent marker."

"Whoa. That's wild." She went to the fridge and pulled out a plastic container, then removed the lid and brought it to the table. "Grapes?"

"Yes, please." He plucked a few from the container, then paused. Her masked expression rankled him. "That look on your face...is there something about my story that bothers you?"

A pink flush crept up her slender neck. She sighed. "Max."

He liked the way she said his name, even in that irritated tone. Like he was familiar to her.

"I believe you. Really, I do." She lined up the forks in the center of the paper napkins she'd folded in half. "But it's kind of a lot. We thought you were—"

"Dead?" He finished the sentence so she didn't have to, then studied her. Is this what the doctor had meant by being prepared for anything? That people who'd known him would wrestle with his reappearance? "I wish I hadn't been gone so long. Or forgotten who I was and the people I loved. And sadly, there's no predictable timeline on when or if I'll regain my memories."

Her eyes welled with tears.

Oh no. His chest tightened. Upsetting her was the last thing he wanted to do.

Clearing her throat, she then blinked away the tears and stood quickly. Someone knocked at the door. Fiona started fussing. He braced his hands on the table to push to his feet, then hesitated. "I don't want to overstep. Do you want to get the door? Or should I hold the baby?"

"I think I should answer the door because seeing you is going to be a real shock. Fiona will be all right for just a minute or two." She brushed past him, and he caught a whiff of a citrus scent. Or maybe it was more like flowers? He couldn't be certain, but he sure liked it. He stood in her wake while Fiona amped up her crying. How was he supposed to sit there and listen and not help? Besides, he knew what to do.

He crossed to the swing, fumbled with the buckles, and then scooped the tiny baby into his arms. She blinked and stared up at him. Her pale blue eyes roamed his face.

"Hey, there," he said softly. Warmth bloomed in his chest. "I'm your—"

"Max Butler." A middle-aged woman holding two plastic bags stood in the house's entryway. She looked like a taller, older version of Hayley. Same green eyes but wore her gray hair short and spiky.

"Hello," he said, snuggling Fiona against his chest.

Hayley stared at him. "What are you doing?"

"I'm holding Fiona."

"She stopped crying."

"Yep." Max grinned, then shifted his attention to the older woman. "Have we met?"

"Max, this is my mom, Donna Morgan." Hayley closed the front door. "We haven't had time to rehash all the details, but he's back."

"I can't believe it." Donna's gaze pinged between him and Hayley. "Amnesia?"

"Sounds that way." Hayley took the grocery bags. The plastic crinkled in her hands. "Thanks for bringing lunch and the diapers. We can eat as soon as you're ready."

Max limped after Hayley as she breezed into the kitchen. "Is there something wrong with me holding her? I mean, we are family."

Hayley bit her lip. "No. No issue. And you're right. You are family." She gave a tight smile and then unloaded the contents of the bags onto the counter. "If you wouldn't mind holding her a few more minutes, I'll warm her bottle."

"Sure." He tried not to grimace as he turned toward the table. His ankle reminded him that he hadn't done anything to address the swelling.

Hayley unwrapped three sub-style sandwiches. "What's wrong with your ankle?"

Max's mouth watered. When had he eaten last? "Pretty sure I sprained it."

"Do you want some ice?"

"Eventually." He clenched his teeth and made his way back to his chair. "Fiona, that's an impressive head of hair you've got there."

He lowered himself into his chair, holding her gently in his arms. Something about her features struck a chord. Again, his brain served up a glitchy signal, but identifying the crucial details remained irritatingly just beyond his grasp. The feeling passed as quickly as it had arrived.

"Here." Hayley pulled out the extra chair beside him at the kitchen table, then quickly folded a kitchen towel into a neat square. "Take your boot off and put your foot up there."

Max hesitated, then shifted into a more comfortable position. Fiona squirmed, protesting the slight jostle. She cried louder. Her face flushed red. "Why don't we get her taken care of, and then we can worry about me?"

Hayley frowned. "All right, but we're putting ice on that ankle. Sooner rather than later."

Max smiled. "Noted. Thank you."

She turned away, tossing her hair off her shoulder. Man, she was cute. And possibly just as strong-willed as the baby he was holding. He couldn't help but stare...until she caught him. They locked eyes. An odd feeling zipped through his chest. He did his best to ignore it. Starting a new relationship was not part of his plan. Not now. Not when he couldn't remember anything about this place or the people who seemed to know so much about him.

Donna grabbed a tissue from the box at the end of the counter and then dabbed at her cheeks. "I was going to hug you," she said, "but you look like you have no idea who I am."

Fiona cried louder, clearly undone by the delay. "Sorry, I don't," Max said. "If somebody could bring me Fiona's bottle? Then we can catch up over lunch."

"It's almost ready." Hayley glanced toward the bottle in the warmer on the counter. "Mom, will you take the sandwiches to the table?"

"Of course." Donna collected the sandwiches, two bags of chips and extra napkins, then sat down across from him. Max's stomach twisted. This was so awkward. He didn't know these women, but judging by their emotional responses, his presence here obviously meant something to them. And the more he scanned his brain, the more his anxiety increased. He could not find one single thread that linked him to Donna. Or Hayley.

A few minutes later, Hayley brought him a bottle. "Do you want me to feed her?"

"No, I've got it. Thanks." Max took the bottle and gently angled it toward Fiona's mouth. She began slurping away like it was the last ounce of formula on the planet. "There we go." He made gentle shushing noises. "That's the way. Well done."

Except for Fiona swallowing her formula, silence hung in the air. He glanced up to find Hayley and Donna staring at him, their mouths slack.

He couldn't resist flashing a triumphant grin. "Big brother to the rescue."

"Be careful," Donna said. "Hayley and Juliet will hire you to take the night shift."

"Deal." Max looked at Hayley. "When do I start?"

Why did Max have to look so good holding Fiona? And why had her mother said that?

"You should probably speak to your dad first." Hayley crumpled her empty sandwich wrapper and shoved it into her empty single-serving chip bag. Salty, crunchy food was always her go-to when she felt stressed. Max coming back to Opportunity had definitely spiked her stress level. Still, she couldn't stop staring. His features had matured into chiseled perfection, and his sandy-blond hair brushed his collar in a way that made her fingers itch to run her hands through it.

As if sensing her gaze, Max looked up and caught her eye. A small smile tugged at his lips before he turned his attention back to Fiona. Ugh. So not fair. It was like he was made to be a big brother. The sight stirred something in her. Something bittersweet. He'd always cared about people, especially kids. No one had been a bigger supporter of her dreams to build an indoor recreation facility than Max. That was why she'd been so shocked when he'd told her to find someone else, and that he never wanted to have a family of his own.

"Cookie?" Mom lifted the lid from a disposable plastic container and then slid it across the table. Her scrumptious chocolate chip cookies stood in neat stacks of four.

"Aw, thank you, Mom. You didn't have to do that."

Mom shrugged then smiled and reached for one. "I wanted to. Max can help you and Juliet finish them."

Max set the empty baby bottle on the table, then carefully lifted Fiona onto his shoulder and patted her back. He flashed Hayley a grin. "Rate me.

Scale of one to ten. How am I doing with feeding and burping her?"

So he was still a shameless flirt. Super. "Seven point five."

His smile faded. "What? Why?"

Hayley refused to answer. Instead, she took a rather aggressive bite of her chocolate chip cookie.

"You seem to know what you're doing, Max," her mother said. "Have you babysat a lot?"

An awkward silence blanketed the table. Max hesitated. Hayley stopped chewing and leaned forward, eager to hear what he had to say. As much as she hated to admit it, she wanted every single detail of the life he'd been living. Without his family. Without her.

"Where I stayed, everybody works together. Caraz is a quiet, close-knit community. They're used to tourists who are climbers, though, so I probably wasn't the first American they'd had to rescue. At first, I couldn't do much because of my headaches and fuzzy vision, but as soon as I was able, I helped look after the kids."

Hayley studied him. "Do you still have blurred vision and headaches?"

Max's forehead furrowed and he looked away. Uh-oh. Had she asked too many questions?

"Sorry. I didn't mean to pry."

"I don't mind answering your questions," Max said quietly. "Sometimes people don't like my answers, though. The blurry vision is mostly gone, and the headaches are intermittent. Eventually I felt well enough to learn to build houses."

"That's not a new skill set. You helped build houses when you were in college."

Max's lips pressed into a thin line. He winced, then rubbed his fingertips across his forehead.

Mom shot her a warning look.

"What? He did."

Guilt crept in. He had been through a lot. But getting used to him being alive and sitting here with gaps in his memory wasn't easy. Especially since he didn't recall how he'd once felt about her. She dabbed at her mouth with her napkin, then met his wounded gaze. "What's the best way for us to fill you in about your past?"

"Little bits at a time. Otherwise, it's overwhelming," he said. "My brain can't file the details away because there's no place to put them."

"Got it."

Except she didn't get it. Not really. A half-dozen questions flitted through her head. She'd save those for later, though.

Fiona burped, then hiccupped. They all chuckled.

Mom dusted the crumbs from her fingers onto her plate, then pushed back her chair and stood. "She is such a cutie. I'd be glad to hold her if the two of you want to go out to the guesthouse and look around." She paused, her gaze pinging between them before landing on Max. "Assuming you'll be moving out there?"

Max repositioned Fiona like a wide receiver tucking a football into the crook of his elbow. "If that's what works best."

"Fiona wakes up frequently and cries loud in the middle of the night. You probably don't want to listen to that." Hayley crossed to the sink and grabbed a paper towel and a bottle of cleaner to wipe down the table. "Besides, Juliet and I have claimed the extra bedrooms upstairs already, so…"

He held up his free hand. "Say no more. Guesthouse it is."

"Great." She squirted the cleaner across the table's faux wood surface and pretended not to notice the muscles in his cheek twitching. Why didn't she feel great about the arrangement? It was the appropriate place for him to settle in. She and Juliet had to be in the main house to take care of Fiona. And it wasn't like they'd been expecting him to come home.

Mom patted his shoulder. "We're so glad you're back, Max. Your family must be thrilled."

Max gently slid Fiona into Donna's outstretched arms. "I haven't reached out yet. I need to, though. Soon."

"Hayley has all their numbers. I'm sure she can get you connected."

Of course. Add "help Max call his father" to

her job description. The knot in her stomach tightened. She turned away so Max couldn't see her expression. Yeah, she should probably feel relieved that a good man once thought gone forever had returned. And she did feel relieved. Mostly. But his presence undid her. And he'd been home less than two hours.

"Let me finish cleaning up, and then I'll take you out to the guesthouse." She pulled open the kitchen drawer at the end of the L-shaped counter. "Here's where we keep the key."

When should she mention that his previous life had been packed away in boxes? Did she risk oversharing about a past he couldn't remember? Max had made it clear that he only wanted small pieces of information at a time.

But his amnesia blurred her emotions.

She couldn't deny her attraction toward him, with his scruffy beard and broad shoulders. And the fact that he took to Fiona so easily only added to his appeal. But she couldn't let herself get carried away. Who knew if he'd stick around? Or if he would ever regain his memories? And how would she cope if he remembered how much they'd once meant to each other but decided he no longer cared about her?

The thought made her shudder. She stuffed the notion deep down as she loaded the dishwasher and wiped down the counter while Mom and Max chatted and tended to Fiona. The baby's eyes were closed. Imagine that. Her mother and Max had met Fiona's needs in a matter of minutes while she struggled with simple tasks.

Maybe accepting this job had been a mistake.

Max stood outside the guesthouse, his breath visible in the frigid air, waiting for Hayley to unlock the door. Shivering, he scanned his surroundings. From the sloped blue metal roof and durable gray exterior to the top-of-the-line windows, he noted that someone had spared no expense building this structure.

"Hopefully there's a winter coat in there that fits." He couldn't stand another minute in these freezing temperatures, especially wearing nothing more than his well-loved cargo pants and a thin T-shirt layered under a hoodie.

"Sorry." Hayley shot him an apologetic look over her shoulder. "The lock sticks sometimes. Just a second."

She jiggled the key again.

He tried not to stare at her petite frame swathed in a puffy gray parka, or the clever way she'd twisted her hair up into a messy bun. He'd sensed tension over lunch. And her curt reminder that she knew more about him than he did felt like a gut punch. He hated having to rely on anyone. For anything. But the last two years and plenty of firm nudges from the Lord had taught him that he required help if he wanted to fully recover. Whatever fully recovered looked like.

"There." The dead bolt slid open with a thunk. She pushed open the door wider and flipped on the lights.

Max followed her inside. Warm, stale air enveloped him. He rubbed his palms together, trying to generate warmth in his cold fingers. He looked around. A large flat-screen TV hung above a cozy fireplace. A plush, comfortable-looking couch and a matching recliner separated the living area from the kitchen, which had a breakfast bar, stainless-steel appliances and quartz countertops.

"This place is amazing," he said.

"Not your typical guesthouse, right?" Hayley shut the door behind him. "We've kept the heat on so the pipes won't freeze. Juliet had planned to stay out here, but like I said earlier, we're both in the house because it's easier to take care of Fiona."

He turned in a slow circle, stopping when he noticed three cardboard boxes and two plastic bins labeled with his name. A mix of apprehension and confusion washed over him. "Wow, this is mine? Did I live here before I left?"

"Rachel told me she packed it up and labeled it for you…before we thought you were…" Hayley paused, twisting the key ring around her finger. "I've heard that your mom and dad couldn't agree about what to do with your stuff, so here it is. Rachel didn't want to donate or throw it away."

"Good to know. Thanks." He rubbed at the familiar ache in his forehead. The same headache resurfaced whenever thoughts about decoding his past overwhelmed him. "I haven't missed any of it."

"But I'm sure there are things you'll need," Hayley said, unzipping her jacket. "Maybe you'll find some clothes that fit in one of these boxes. I mean, I don't want to tell you what to do or anything."

"Oh, come on, sure you do."

Her cheeks flushed at his words. But she didn't smile back.

Uh-oh. His teasing had fallen flat. Maybe jokes weren't the best way to ease the tension between them.

"I'm just trying to help you, Max. Coming back, declaring to your hometown that you aren't actually dead, finding out you have a little sister—seems like a lot for one person to deal with."

He nodded slowly, taking in her words. "Hayley, I was just joking around. I know you're trying to help. Thank you." He paused and then added with a sheepish grin, "I do need a warmer jacket."

"If my mom will stay with Fiona, I can help you look for one. Your dad probably has something in his closet that will fit."

It made sense that she'd know where he might find what he needed to start over here. Maybe he should take her advice and talk with his dad before he did anything else. But that required calling the father who didn't know he was alive. It seemed like a phone call he should make, but something had been keeping him from reaching out. Something warned him that that would be a tough conversation. He'd worry about all that later.

"I'll think about it. Is the bedroom back here?" He turned away from the boxes, skirted the couch and walked through a cased opening. "Whoa."

A king-size bed flanked with two oak nightstands took up the opposite wall. A wide window overlooked the snow-covered backyard. The whole room had been painted a calming shade of green-gray.

"There's a full bath with a small linen closet through that door," Hayley said. "They had this place remodeled because Rachel's mom was going to stay here, but then she fell and hurt her back and needed surgery. So Juliet and I stepped up. At least until Rachel gets the help she needs, and her mom gets back on her feet."

Max noted the closed bathroom door, then walked over and examined the gorgeous built-in bookshelves beside the window. He ran his hand over the smooth woodwork. "Do you think Rachel will feel well enough to come home soon?"

"I don't know." Sighing, Hayley leaned against the dresser. "Her emotions were rather volatile, and she just couldn't care for Fiona and herself. Your dad thought it was best that she gets some professional help, and the place that would take her and that insurance would pay for is out of state."

"So no official timeline on her return?"

"We're hoping six weeks. Honestly, Juliet and I are hoping for sooner. Fiona is a wreck without her mother, but we'll do the best we can. Your dad is expected back sometime next week."

"I'm glad you and your sister can take care of her. I don't have a job yet. If there's something I can do to help, please let me know," Max said.

Hayley grinned. "You're going to regret saying that."

Finally. He'd coaxed a genuine smile out of her. And a warmth filled her eyes that felt like a ray of sunshine splitting wide a grim stormy sky. Sure, things had been a little tense between them. But he was grateful for her presence and her help. Even if the stubborn part of him bristled at the thought of needing extra assistance.

"It's a sincere offer." He tucked his hands in the front pocket of his hoodie. "If I'm going to live here, I need to contribute."

Something undecipherable flickered in her eyes. "All right. Agreed. When Juliet comes over later, we can work out a schedule for taking care of Fiona. I left my phone on the counter in the main house. We should probably get back and see if my mom's all right with her. You need to ice and elevate that ankle too."

"Right."

As he followed her back outside, Max couldn't shake the feelings tugging at him. His past was a mystery that he was hesitant to unravel, but he couldn't ignore the questions that lingered at the edge of his consciousness. And he wanted to get well. To recover from his head trauma and get back to climbing mountains again. Still, he was torn. Torn between wanting to know more about himself and dreading what painful memories might resurface.

Chapter Three

Unease skated through Hayley as she drove from the Butlers' house to the physical therapy clinic early Monday morning. She had never asked her manager to evaluate a patient for free. But then again, she'd never known a man with amnesia who she'd once been in love with and had more than likely sprained his ankle. She stole a glance at Max sitting next to her in the passenger seat. Poor guy. She couldn't let him suffer.

She slowed as she passed the vacant lot where she'd dreamed of building an indoor recreational facility someday. A brand-new For Sale sign hung from a sturdy post near the street.

Hayley sucked in a breath. How had she not heard about this already?

"Everything okay?" Max eyed her, his curious gaze warming her skin.

"Yeah. I'm just surprised to see that sign." She sped up, keeping her focus on the street. "I've had my eye on that land for a while. The family that owns it said they wouldn't sell, though. Guess they changed their mind."

"What do you want to build?"

Sighing, she tapped the turn signal and headed for the clinic. He'd forgotten all about her dream. Their dream. Was this really happening?

"I have this wild idea to build an indoor recreation center. A large facility that kids and grown-ups can use to play sports, exercise, swim all year round." Hayley parked in front of the building, then turned off the ignition.

"Wow." Max released a low whistle. "That sounds fantastic."

"Yeah, well, I'd need a large piece of land and more than a million dollars. Both of which I'm currently lacking. It's just a dream at this point."

One we worked on together, by the way.

Max tipped his head toward the clinic. "What made you choose physical therapy?"

She held back a frustrated sigh. He'd known all of this once. He'd been the first person she'd told when she got accepted to the program in Anchorage. "I wanted a good job with a great salary so I could support myself, and I tried to avoid spending a ton of time or money on my education. A physical therapist has to get a PhD now, but an assistant can be in and out of school in five semesters."

"Makes sense." Max gestured to the to-go cups

of coffee, nestled in the center console of her SUV. "Can I carry something for you?"

"Sure. Thanks." She quickly got out of the car, wincing as the frigid air greeted her. Temperatures had dropped overnight, hinting at the impending storm expected to dump at least six inches of snow. She reached behind the seat, collected her backpack, then slung it over her shoulder and made her way toward the clinic.

Inside, the clinic's receptionist, Annabelle, stood behind the front desk, purse and keys still in her hand as she powered up the computer.

"Good morning," Hayley greeted her with a smile.

Annabelle's long, silky black hair brushed her shoulders as she took off her jacket. Her brown eyes slid to Max as he limped in after Hayley. "Sir, we're not open yet."

"It's okay, he's with me," Hayley reassured her, pausing in front of the desk. "This is my friend, Max Butler. Max, this is Annabelle."

Annabelle's dark brows scrunched together. "But I don't have anyone named Max Butler on the schedule."

Guilt pinched her insides. Maybe she should've texted Annabelle to let her know Max was coming in. "I know it's last minute, but I'm hoping we can squeeze him onto Garrett's schedule. He's had an accident, and I'm afraid he sprained his ankle. I'll speak to Garrett and explain all the details. Max, if you'll have a seat right here, we'll be with you shortly."

"Yeah, sure." Max turned toward the row of four blue plastic chairs pushed up against the wall in the small waiting area.

"Does he need new patient paperwork?" Annabelle asked.

"Most likely, yes." Hayley plucked her coffee from the cardboard carrier Max had brought in.

"I don't expect to be treated any differently just because of my unusual circumstances," Max said.

"But your circumstances are unusual," Hayley said. "Which is why I'm offering to help. I do have to ask my manager for permission. So if you wouldn't mind sitting here while I check with him, that would be great."

He nodded, then took the clipboard Annabelle handed him and collected a pen from the cup on the counter.

Hayley strode down the corridor and across the empty gym area where they prescribed exercises for their patients. She went into the break room. Garrett stood at the refrigerator, putting his lunch away.

He glanced up and offered a polite smile. "Good morning."

"Hey, Garrett. Do you have a minute? I've got a situation."

"Oh? Starting our Monday off with some excitement, I see. What can I do to help?"

She set down her coffee and backpack. "I don't think you lived here yet, but a couple of years ago, a local guy named Max Butler went missing in Peru. Have you heard his story?"

Garrett nodded. "Bits and pieces. He was a mountain climber, right?"

"Right. He took teams up to Denali all the time. He's been missing, presumed dead, but…now he's back and he has retrograde amnesia. I'm pretty sure he sprained his ankle too. Is there any way that we could treat him? He doesn't have a job, so no insurance yet. Other than what I just told you, plus some basic information about his recent health history, we don't have a lot of details to work with."

"Wow. Okay." Garrett rubbed his palms together. "Does he have any special skills?"

Thoughts of him holding Fiona filtered through her head. She quickly banished them. "Other than mountain climbing? Maybe. He can build houses. What did you have in mind?"

Garrett hesitated. "Let me meet the guy first. When can he come in?"

"He's in the waiting room."

"Perfect. I don't have a patient until nine fifteen, so I'll take him back now."

"Awesome. Thank you for doing this." She hung up her coat, quickly stashed her bag under her desk in their shared workspace, then walked with Garrett back out to the waiting room.

"Max, this is my manager, Garrett Johnson. Garrett, my friend, Max Butler," Hayley said.

Grinning, Max set the pen and clipboard aside, then stood and shook Garrett's outstretched hand. "Nice to meet you, Garrett. You've got a cool setup here."

"Thank you." Garrett glanced around. "We're bursting at the seams and hoping to expand this spring. Hayley says you may have injured your ankle recently?"

Max glanced down at his feet. "Yes, sir. Injured it in the Dallas airport."

"I'm sorry to hear that," Garrett said. "Why don't you bring the paperwork with you and come on back? We'll have a look."

"Appreciate it." Max smiled at Hayley as he moved past her, then followed Garrett into the nearest exam room.

Hayley came in behind him. Man, he smelled good. His hair, still damp from the shower, brushed the collar of his black puffer jacket.

"Filled that out as best as I could but left a lot of stuff blank." Max set down the clipboard and took a seat on one of the exam tables. The paper covering crinkled under his weight. "I don't know the answers."

Oh, Max. Hayley's heart pinched, and she quickly tucked the clipboard under her arm. "Don't worry about it."

Max slipped off his boot, peeled off his sock

and scooted back so Garrett could take a closer look. "I bought an ankle brace yesterday at the sporting goods store, but my ankle's too swollen to wear it."

"That's to be expected." Garrett nudged a four-wheeled stool closer to the end of the table and sat down.

Hayley stood back, eyeing the deep purple discoloration. After asking several questions and gently examining Max's lower leg and ankle, Garrett pushed back his stool. "Typically we get authorization to treat a patient from a referral. A physician at the ER, or a nurse practitioner from a medical clinic. A comprehensive exam also includes an X-ray."

Max frowned. "So you want me to see a doctor and get an X-ray?"

"Not necessarily," Garrett said. "In my opinion, I don't think you need an X-ray because I don't believe you broke your ankle. If you agree, we can start treating you." Garrett glanced up at Hayley. "I'll hand him off to you for the usual protocol—control swelling, manage the pain and gradually increase his range of motion. Then we'll progress to strengthening as tolerated."

"Got it." Hayley clasped her hands in front of her. Sure, okay, this had been her idea to bring Max here. But she'd hoped Garrett would take care of the treatment himself. Not pass him off to her.

"This sounds great, but I don't have a job or insurance," Max said.

Garrett looked thoughtful. "Since this is an unconventional arrangement, I have an unconventional proposition."

Max grinned. "Unconventional is kind of my thing."

Then he smiled at Hayley, and it was all she could do not to flush from the neckline of her polo shirt to the roots of her hair.

Stop. It.

She quickly looked away, silently praying that Garrett wouldn't notice. She shifted awkwardly from one foot to the other, waiting for Garrett to elaborate.

"Like I said earlier, as soon as the weather warms up, we're going to knock down a wall or two and expand this place. We're not busy right this minute, but when Hayley, myself, the other therapist and the PT aide are all in here, it's crowded. I'd love to expand so we can treat more patients. Something tells me you're the man for the job."

"We're trading? Ankle sprain treatment in exchange for…carpentry?" Max's expression grew serious. "Are you sure I'm qualified?"

"Not 100 percent," Garrett said. "But I'm willing to give you a chance. By the time I get the general contractor in here, I'm sure Hayley will have your pain under control, your mobility back and you'll be ready to work. What do you say?"

Max looked at Hayley. "Is this okay with you?"

"Of course." She infused her voice with a confidence she didn't yet feel. Max could still fluster her. Could she handle living next door to him, caring for Fiona together and treating his injury? How in the world would she resist his charm?

"You have my word that we'll help you rehab that ankle, and hopefully get you ready to climb again. Then when the time is right, I'll need your help expanding our clinic. Deal?" Garrett offered his hand.

Without hesitating, Max sealed the deal with a handshake. "I'd like to get this ankle back to where it needs to be. Denali certainly caught my attention when I rolled into town."

Hayley's heart lurched. "Y-you want to climb Denali again?"

Garrett shot her a surprised look.

Max's gaze slid from Garrett to her. "Maybe. Probably. I'd be lying if I said a mountain like that wasn't on my radar. My endurance has tanked, and I lost my confidence after that fall. I'm not even sure I remember how to climb."

"Let's get your ankle squared away, then you can progress to your normal activities." Garrett stood and pushed the stool out of the way.

"When do I get started with my treatment?"

"Right now," Garrett said. "I'll let Annabelle know that Max is Hayley's first patient of the day, and she'll adjust your schedule accordingly."

"Great. Thanks," Hayley said, offering Garrett a tight-lipped smile to mask her uncertainty. Then drew a calming breath. Did Max even know what he was saying? Sure, he'd skimmed over the details of his accident—which she'd assumed was because he still didn't know a whole lot about what had happened. But hadn't he been clear that climbing had caused his trauma? So why would he want to put himself in harm's way again?

Dread pooled in her stomach. This was so not what she'd expected when she'd offered to help Max.

He should've called his mom sooner.

Max set the phone he'd borrowed from Juliet on the coffee table, then slowly sank back against the couch cushions. Hayley had shared his mother's phone number and even offered to call her first and gently let her know he'd come home. But he'd insisted he could handle it. He couldn't let Hayley break the news to his mother. It was his responsibility. Still, he'd been so nervous to call. There wasn't exactly a step-by-step manual for letting a parent know their kid had turned up alive.

The instant she'd heard his voice, though, she'd burst into tears. It had taken a minute for her to form coherent sentences. His chest tightened. Maybe he should've accepted Hayley's suggestion and let her or Juliet call first and give Mom a heads-up. Because even after he'd explained about his traumatic injury, memory loss and his time spent in Peru, Mom still sounded like she was in shock. Maybe even a little jealous that he'd chosen Opportunity instead of showing up on her doorstep. After all, she was thousands of miles away from here in Montana.

He'd struggled to find the words to explain that he didn't know her, much less how to find out where she lived. Sighing, he scrubbed his hand over his face, then rearranged the ice bags he'd sandwiched around his ankle before he'd called his mom. This morning's physical therapy session with Hayley had been intense. She'd empathized with his discomfort but held firm in her expectations. He respected her professionalism, yet sort of missed the more casual version of Hayley he'd encountered first. Maybe her all-business approach was exactly what he needed, though. Yeah, the range of motion exercises were a challenge, but he mostly felt relieved to be addressing the pain and swelling issues. Garrett's offer to barter for his treatment in exchange for working on the construction project later had been a blessing. God had really shown up in ways that Max had not expected.

"How was your phone call?" Juliet came in from the kitchen, carrying Fiona in her arms.

"It was all right," Max said. "Better than expected, but I feel guilty."

"Why?"

"My mom was shocked, of course, which is understandable. Also a little disappointed that she hadn't heard from me sooner. It was hard to explain that calling a stranger and trying to convince her I'm her missing son wasn't something I was comfortable with. But now I'm worried I might've hurt her feelings because she can't quite wrap her mind around the fact that I don't have any memories of her."

Empathy filled Juliet's eyes. "I'm glad you called her, even though it was probably scary."

"Yeah, me too. She said something about looking at flights. She wants to visit soon." Max gestured to the phone. "Thanks for loaning me your phone. Hopefully, I'll get one this week. With no recent credit history and barely any identity at all, it's hard accessing things that most people take for granted."

Juliet scrunched up her nose. "Wow, I can't even imagine what you've been through or what you'll be dealing with over the next few months. We're glad that you're here, Max, and we'll help you however we can."

Fiona started crying.

"Thank you." Max shifted his position, eager to change the subject. One phone call today was enough. He would put off calling his dad until tomorrow. "How's Fiona?"

"Cranky." Juliet glanced at the baby. "Between the hours of four and seven seem to be the worst."

"Really? Why?"

"We don't know. She cries quite a bit. I'm sure we've mentioned that at least ten times since you've come home."

"Here." Max held out his arms. "Let me take her."

Juliet hesitated. "You don't know what you're offering."

"I'm just sitting here, icing my ankle for another ten minutes, so let me hold her. It will give you a break."

"Thanks. Hayley should be here soon. We tag-team the evening responsibilities."

"Now you can split the work three ways."

Juliet gently handed Fiona over.

"Hey, pretty girl," Max said. Fiona stared up at him and dialed back the crying. He nestled her against his chest and carefully supported her with his arm. Then he adjusted the pink-and-white-polka-dotted blanket and breathed in her sweet smell. It was like powder or lotion or something. "She sure is a cutie."

"She has her moments. I try to remind myself to cut her some slack. She's only three months old and she must be missing her parents." Her phone hummed on the coffee table. "Let me get that." Juliet picked up the phone and glanced at the screen. "Oh, cool. Hayley says she'll be here in a few minutes, and she has Jill from the Sluice Box with her."

Max patiently waited for more of an explanation.

"Oh, right. Sorry." Juliet laughed nervously. "The Sluice Box is a restaurant in town. Hayley worked there as a server for a while, and you were one of their most loyal customers."

"Wow, really? I wish I remembered. It's so weird not to have memories of any of that."

"When the owners heard you were back, they offered to bring food by." Juliet swiped her finger across the screen. "Hayley says they'll be here in five minutes."

"They don't have to do that."

"Jill and her brother Danny are super kind. They have the biggest hearts. To be honest, if I were you, I wouldn't turn away the meal. Hayley and I can take care of Fiona, but cooking isn't our gift."

Max laughed. "Understood."

A few minutes later, the door opened and Hayley came in. Fresh snow coated her green knit hat and clung to her jacket. "Hi there."

"Hey." Warmth bloomed in his chest. Interesting. For a guy with memory loss, he sure was happy to see her. Confusion immediately seeped in, though. How did he know Hayley? Had this restaurant that Juliet mentioned been their only connection? Or was there something deeper between them that he couldn't remember? He forced a smile and pushed down his conflicted thoughts. He'd have to ask her later about their history. If they even had one.

"Max, you have a visitor." Hayley smiled and angled her head toward the middle-aged blonde who stepped inside, her arms loaded with two brown paper bags. "This is Jill."

The woman's blue eyes filled with tears. "Oh, Max. I can't believe it," she said, her voice thick with emotion. "This is amazing! I'm so happy to see you again."

"Hi, Jill." Max offered a polite smile that he hoped masked his discomfort. He didn't know what to say. Her happiness seemed genuine, but he couldn't help feeling awkward and out of place.

Hayley took off her coat and hat, and then she took the bags of food, her gaze pinging between him and Jill. "Would you like to join us, Jill?"

"Oh, no, thank you. I don't want to impose. Besides, I need to get back to the restaurant." She swiped at the moisture on her cheeks, then gave Max another wobbly smile. "It's good to see you again, Max. When you feel like having more visitors, I know Danny would love to say hello."

Before he could answer, Fiona fussed and squirmed in his arms. Max slid his foot from the ice and then gingerly stood, wincing at the pain.

"You good, Max?" Juliet took the bags from Hayley, then paused, pinning him with a concerned look. "Or do you want me to take her?"

"If she doesn't stop crying, I'll try putting her in the swing," he said.

"Thanks again for feeding us," Hayley said. "And please tell Danny he's welcome to stop by."

"Sounds good." Jill turned to leave, but then whirled around and clasped Hayley's arm. "Oh, I almost forgot. I'm serving on the nominating committee for this year's Spring Fling. We need six couples in the royal court. I'd love to nominate you and Max. Wouldn't that be fun? Just like old times, right?"

Fiona cried louder. Max shifted her onto his shoulder and took a few steps, eager to soothe her discomfort. His ankle protested, but he kept moving. Selfishly, he wanted to get closer to hear the rest of Jill and Hayley's conversation.

"I—I don't think so, Jill." Hayley reached around her and opened the door. "Max just got back and I'm swamped."

"I get that." Jill tugged her keys from her pocket. "But you two were so cute together when—"

"Thanks again for dinner." Hayley patted Jill's shoulder and then ushered her onto the porch. "Talk soon."

She closed the door, locked the dead bolt and turned toward him. As she tugged her boots off, she asked, "How are you feeling? Any memories coming back?"

"Sadly, no. I did speak to my mom. Thanks for helping me connect with her."

"No problem." Hayley took an elastic band from her wrist and twisted her hair into a ponytail.

Max averted his gaze. The last thing he needed was for Hayley to catch him staring. He crossed to the baby swing and carefully lowered Fiona into the cushioned seat, fumbling with the clasps until he managed to buckle her in.

"She likes the setting that sounds like the ocean." Hayley padded across the room. She reached up and pushed a few buttons on the swing's plastic frame. A sound that mimicked waves rolling onto shore played through the speaker. "There."

He stared at Fiona, willing her to stop crying so he and Hayley could finish this conversation. Thankfully, her fussing morphed into something that resembled a gurgle. Or maybe a happy coo.

"How about that." Max gently nudged Hayley with his elbow. "She looks like she might smile."

Hayley's mouth drifted open. "I—I can't believe it."

Max studied her. "What was Jill talking about?"

"Nothing." A muscle in Hayley's cheek twitched. She refused to look at him.

"It didn't sound like nothing. And you rushed her right out the door."

Hayley's cheeks turned an adorable shade of pink. "The Spring Fling is an annual event held in March. It's partly for entertainment, but there's also a fundraising component. Six men and six women are nominated to serve—" she paused to make air quotes "—the 'royal court,' but there's nothing royal or official about it. Typically, the nominated couples commit to showing up at various events around town. For example, we might be asked to serve cocoa while everyone celebrates the ice on the river breaking up or help coordinate a bingo game at the community center. Sometimes the couples can't take time off from work, so they help decorate for the dance. At the end of the week, there's a semiformal dance where the king and queen are chosen."

"Sounds fun." Max shoved his hands in his back pockets. "What's the fundraising for?"

A strand of hair slipped from her ponytail. Hayley tucked it behind her ear. "In the past, kids who wanted to travel out-of-state for sports camps or attend a national convention for their school club had to pay for hotel and plane tickets, so we've fundraised for that. Sometimes nonprofit organizations like the food pantry fundraise to cover operating expenses. The booths at the Spring Fling don't generate a lot of money, but every little bit helps. People are already out and about, guessing when the ice is cracking, so maybe they're feeling extra generous and eager to support important causes."

"Based on what you told me about your dream of building a venue for kids' activities, this event sounds like something you'd support. Maybe even use it to spotlight your passion project. So if the Spring Fling benefits the community, why did you tell her no?"

Hayley winced. The silence hung heavy between them. Then she crossed her arms and tipped her chin up. "Because I was already nominated a few years ago. We both were. And neither one of us needs to take on more responsibility."

Oh. That wasn't the answer he'd expected. He rubbed his fingers along his jaw. "I see. Thank you. I do have another question if you don't mind."

She hesitated. "Okay."

"When I lived here before, did you and I have some sort of...connection? I mean, other than me eating at Jill's restaurant where you worked. Like, did we hang out, or..."

"You know what? I'm starving. Let's eat before the food gets cold." Hayley turned and headed into the kitchen. "Juliet, what's in those bags?"

Juliet stared wide-eyed at Hayley. Something he couldn't quite identify passed between the sisters. Then the moment vanished as Juliet set more containers on the counter. "Beef stew, fresh-baked bread and chocolate chip cheesecake. It's scrumptious, by the way, so save room for dessert."

A hollow ache settled behind his sternum as he crossed to the refrigerator and grabbed a soda. That hadn't been a real response, and to be honest, a part of him had hoped she'd say they had a friendship that went beyond their interactions at the restaurant. But maybe he'd misread her kindness. Maybe he just wanted to feel connected to this place and the people who'd once been a part of his life. But Hayley was probably right—volunteering at a festival wasn't the best use of his time. Especially since he'd just committed to helping take care of Fiona and work on a substantial construction project at the PT clinic.

He popped the top on the soda and took a long drink, trying to ease his disappointment. His mind raced with questions, but he wasn't sure he wanted to know the answers. Was he just a former customer or a guy with an ankle sprain to her? And why did that thought bother him so much?

Chapter Four

Hayley divided the fresh batch of popcorn into two blue and red enamel bowls. "Here." She nudged the saltshaker toward Juliet. "I'll let you add your own salt and butter."

"Oh, this smells good." Juliet reached for the red bowl. "Thank you."

"You're welcome." Hayley drizzled melted butter over her popcorn and then added salt. "Ready to watch the game?"

Juliet nodded, then scooped up a handful of popcorn.

Hayley grabbed two cans of lemon-lime soda from the fridge and carried her snack and the drinks into the living room.

Juliet set her bowl on the coffee table. "Did you invite Max to watch?"

Hayley claimed one end of the sofa. "Nope." With Max in the guesthouse, she could finally relax. Juliet shot her a sideways glance as she reached for the remote control. "Because you're avoiding him?"

The soda can slipped from her hand. Hayley caught it before it landed on her toes. "I'm not avoiding him."

"You're avoiding his questions, though. Why didn't you answer him when he asked if the two of you had a connection?"

Hayley's mouth ran dry. As soon as she'd sidestepped Max's questions in favor of eating the food Jill had brought, she'd sensed Juliet's disapproval. But Max had stunned her with his sudden interest in the Spring Fling royal court, and pushing back on her decision not to participate. He'd barely been home forty-eight hours, and already he got to weigh in on how she volunteered her time?

That wasn't fair.

Rather than snap at her sister, Hayley opened her drink and took a sip. The sweet, carbonated liquid didn't do much to quench her thirst, though. Flames snapped and crackled in the fireplace as Juliet found the football game on TV. She muted the volume, then sat back on the sofa, her bowl of popcorn nestled in her lap. The video baby monitor stationed nearby showed Fiona sleeping in her crib in the nursery upstairs.

"Can't we just watch the game? I don't want to talk about this."

With Max holed up in the guesthouse just yards away, it was far too easy for her thoughts to wander back to him. Frankly, it was emotionally exhausting. She still couldn't wrap her mind around the fact that he'd returned.

"I'm just trying to help," Juliet said. "Before you get yourself in a pickle."

Too late. Hayley scooped up another handful of popcorn and didn't respond.

"Max wants to know about his past, and you're a key component of the memories he's missing." Juliet opened her soda. "You can't conceal the facts forever."

"I'm not concealing anything. He has amnesia, Juliet. Besides, why do I have to be the one who tells him everything?"

Even as the words left her lips, she knew they sounded ridiculous. Almost like a petulant child shifting the blame. But she plowed on with more excuses. "He said he only wants information about his past a little at a time. Lots of detail is too overwhelming so—"

"Except he asked you specifically and you avoided answering him."

"What do you want me to say? That I had a massive crush on him for months, and right when I thought our friendship had grown into something more, something that felt like it might be a permanent partnership, he crushed me with a big, fat 'no thank you'?"

The back door closed, and Max walked into the room, fresh snow dusting the puffy black jacket he'd borrowed from his father's closet. "You both should be proud of me." He offered a sheepish grin. "I was about to announce my entry with a loud yell, then I remembered there might be a sleeping baby."

Hayley's heart pounded, battering her ribs. She gave Juliet a panicked look. What had he heard?

Juliet's mouth formed an alarmed O before she recovered and offered him a bright smile. "We're so proud. Thank you for not waking her."

Hayley dragged her gaze to meet his. "So what's up?"

His cheeks flushed. He cut an uneasy gaze between the sisters. "Am I interrupting something?"

"Nope."

"Uh-uh."

They both shook their heads. At least they agreed on that.

Doubt flitted across his features. Then he glanced at the TV. "How's the game?"

"We're not really watching," Juliet said.

"But it's the playoffs, and Seattle's up by six."

"It's probably on at your place too," Hayley said.

"You're welcome to watch here, though," Juliet added. "There's plenty of popcorn left. Want some?"

"Sure."

And just like that, he was back in the room, taking up space. Hayley pressed her lips closed to keep from saying anything else. This house did belong to his family after all. He had every right to hang out and watch whatever he wanted. Plus, she and Juliet could definitely use his help with Fiona.

Max unlaced his boots, left them by the door, then crossed the room and sank into the recliner by the fireplace. He looked around. "Where is Fiona?"

"Taking her post dinner nap," Hayley said.

"Does she do that a lot?" Max asked.

Hayley nodded, then cast him a quick glance. "You should put your feet up, by the way. Do you need some more ice?"

He grinned at her. "Are you always on?"

"What?"

"You know." He shrugged. "Always on task."

She bit back another sharp retort. Being sassy wouldn't change anything. But how did he manage to get under her skin so quickly? "It's just a suggestion. If you're going to sit there, you might as well put your feet up and ice that ankle."

Hayley wiped her hands on a napkin, then tugged the basket full of clean laundry closer. She plucked one of Fiona's tiny white onesies with an adorable floral pattern and neatly folded it. Rachel might have been struggling with postpartum health issues, but she had certainly outfitted her daughter in some super-adorable clothes.

"I'll get the ice." Juliet headed for the kitchen. "Do you want anything to drink, Max?"

"Just water, please."

Juliet paused in the doorway. "Hayley, do you want more popcorn?"

"I'm good. Thanks." She folded another pair of Fiona's pajamas and added it to the stack of clean stuff on the cushion beside her. Max could tease her all he wanted about getting chores done. His opinion didn't matter. Besides, multitasking kept her going.

Hayley handed Max the remote. "Feel free to turn up the volume."

"Thanks." His callused fingertips brushed against hers, sending goose bumps dancing along her arm. She turned away. He couldn't know how she truly felt. Besides, those feelings were all in the past. Right?

He really hated to ask for another favor. Hayley and Juliet had already done so much. But after speaking to his mother for the first time, he was sort of dreading calling his dad. Without any memories, he was in over his head when it came to navigating family dynamics.

"Here you go." Juliet came in with a bag of ice in one hand and a glass of water in the other. "I'll be right back with your popcorn. If I add enough butter and salt, maybe that will make up for icing your ankle."

"Ice matters," Hayley said, sending her sister a mock scowl. "It helps reduce swelling, which decreases pain and—"

"Yeah, yeah, we know." Juliet smiled, then set the water on the side table beside the recliner. "But it still isn't a pleasant experience. Bring him that blanket, will you?"

Max shifted in the leather chair. "You don't have to do that, Hayley."

Juliet paused and tipped her head sideways. "Let us pamper you. You've been through a lot."

He turned his attention back to the football game on television. She wasn't wrong.

"Here." Hayley tapped a button on a small remote, which caused the recliner's footrest to elevate slowly. She deftly lifted his foot then slipped a pillow underneath his heel. "Extra elevation."

"Thanks," he said, warmth creeping up his neck. All this attention made him nervous.

"I'll let you handle the ice on the ankle." Juliet passed her sister the bag of ice. "You're the professional."

Hayley molded the plastic bag around his swollen ankle. Max sucked in a breath. Even through his sock, the initial contact with the ice was jarring. She avoided eye contact as she awkwardly layered the blanket over his lower body.

"I'll turn up the volume on the game so you can hear the commentary," Hayley said. She traded the chair's remote for the one controlling the TV and then bumped up the sound.

"Wait. Before we get into the game, can I ask you both some questions about my parents?"

Hayley's eyes widened. She quickly turned away and reached for another piece of laundry from the basket.

"You can ask," Juliet said. "We'll do our best to answer, but..." She trailed off, then shook her head. "You're going to need a soda and more popcorn. It's a messy situation. Hang on."

Before he could protest, Juliet returned to the kitchen. A knot settled low in his stomach. How messy? He munched on a handful of popcorn, his mind churning with possible scenarios. An affair? Financial stress? Job loss? He pushed all those thoughts aside. Without any context, he didn't want to make wild guesses. So he'd just have to rely on Hayley and Juliet to offer their insight.

Juliet hustled back with a can of cola and another bowl of popcorn. She offered him the drink.

"Thank you." He popped the top and took a sip.

Juliet settled on the couch with her popcorn. "So, your parents. How much do you want to know?"

"Juliet." Hayley shot her a look. "You don't have to say it quite like that."

Confusion flitted across Juliet's features. "Say it like what? He obviously needs answers, and I don't see anybody else stepping up to fill him in."

Hayley folded a baby blanket into a neat square. "Was your mom happy to hear from you?" she asked him.

Nodding, Max set the can aside and scooped up

another handful of popcorn. "She was. And she told me she's going to come visit as soon as she gets her time off from work approved. Hopefully getting together will shake loose some memories, but I don't know what to do with her. Has she been gone a long time?"

Hayley opened her mouth to answer, but Juliet beat her to it. "She moved away right before you left for Peru."

"I'm guessing she doesn't have a house here anymore?"

"Whoa, look!" Juliet pointed to the TV. "Seattle's about to score a touchdown."

Max bit back a frustrated growl. He loved sports, sensed he always had, but right now he needed details.

Hayley nudged the laundry basket aside and sat down. Her guarded expression softened as she met his gaze. "No. She sold it."

"Do I have aunts and uncles? Cousins?"

"Not here." Juliet muted the volume on the television again. "Your grandparents live in a cabin a little bit closer to Anchorage, though."

"Got it." Max reached for his soda again. "Do I need to call them, too?"

Hayley picked up her bowl and carefully selected a few kernels of popcorn. "They're your mom's parents. Maybe you should ask her."

"Right." More questions were stacking up. "I'm

guessing my mom can't stay here when she comes to visit."

"No, she cannot," Hayley said. "You are right about that."

Juliet and Hayley exchanged glances. "I don't think she'll expect you to handle her arrangements. She still has friends here."

"I just want to know what I'm dealing with," he said quietly.

"It was a really messy divorce," Hayley said.

"Lots of drama," Juliet added.

Max's head began to hurt. He squeezed his eyes shut.

"Uh-oh," Juliet said. "Are you okay?"

He opened his eyes and blew out a long breath.

"Max?" Hayley studied him. "What's happening?"

"Headache," he said, gritting his teeth. Why was this so hard? Why did it all have to be so complicated? Why couldn't he just remember?

"This has got to be super overwhelming," Hayley said. "Why don't we just stick to the basics? Your parents got divorced. Your dad remarried Rachel very quickly. Now they have Fiona. Your mom's been in Montana for a couple of years. Hopefully, she can visit you and head home before your dad and Rachel get back."

"That would probably be for the best," Juliet said.

"Right. Got it." Max massaged his aching forehead with his fingertips. "So I'll need to figure out how to be happy to see a woman that I don't remember. And then make sure to usher her right back out of town before my dad comes home. Who, by the way, has a baby with his new wife, who's struggling with postpartum depression."

An awkward silence filled the room.

"We did try to warn you that it was messy," Hayley said.

"Messy?" Max shook his head. "This sounds like a disaster."

Maybe the reentry into his old life wasn't going to be all that easy. But what was he supposed to do? Stay away forever? Randomly climbing mountains and leading expeditions, then picking up odd jobs to make ends meet? The old Max might've been into that nomadic lifestyle. But sitting here in this cozy house, watching the game, getting to know his baby sister and reconnecting with Hayley and Juliet made him think that there was hope for something more. Something better. Something that truly felt like home.

The next day, after work, Hayley sat alone at the kitchen table in the Butlers' house and scrolled through a set of grant application instructions.

"That's a lot of information," she said to herself, sagging against the ladder-back chair. Community impact data, proof of nonprofit status, budget outlines. Plus, she'd need to update her business plan.

Groaning, she buried her face in her hands and tried to push back a wave of disappointment. She wanted to build this venue, but every single step felt like…well, like trying to summit Denali.

Her phone hummed with an incoming text message. She glanced at the screen.

Hey. It's me. I was just thinking about you today and wondering how you're doing.

"Weston?" She pressed her fingers to her lips. He hadn't messaged her since he moved to California last summer. Yeah, okay, so maybe she'd scrolled through his social media posts a few times to see if he'd started dating someone new. Didn't everyone check up on their exes now and then? But she'd never reached out because she wasn't the least bit interested in a long-distance relationship.

"What's wrong?"

She yelped in surprise. Her phone slipped from her hands and fell on the table. She left it face down and glanced over her shoulder.

Max stood in the doorway, wearing a red-white-and-blue plaid button-down shirt over a red T-shirt. He jammed his hands in the back pockets of his faded jeans.

"Your ankle must be feeling better if you can wear those." She pointed to the leather-and-canvas hiking boots on his feet. "Has your swelling decreased?"

He shrugged. "A little bit. I can't tie the laces supertight yet."

"I'm glad you're making progress."

"You and your team at the clinic deserve the credit." His expression softened. "I wouldn't have recovered this quickly on my own."

She shrugged a shoulder. "It's what we do."

"But you didn't answer my question. What happened to you? Were you crying?"

Hayley sighed. "I wasn't crying. I'm just frustrated. Someone suggested I apply for a grant to help with the start-up costs of building that recreational venue I told you about. I thought it would be easy." She gestured toward her laptop. "But based on the instructions, I need to prepare a ton of information first."

She left out the part about her ex-boyfriend texting her. Max didn't need to know everything.

Max crossed the room and pulled out a chair across from her. As he sat, the pleasant aroma of his aftershave or soap or something teased her senses.

"What kind of information?"

She angled her laptop toward him. "Read for yourself."

He scanned the screen, then frowned. "You're right. That's a lot."

Hayley drew the laptop closer, then shut the lid. She'd have to come up with another plan because a grant sounded outside the realm of possibilities. At least for now.

"So that's it?" Max crossed his arms over his broad chest. "You've hit a dead end and you're not going to try anymore?"

She bristled. Was he serious? "Max, we've talked about this. I know you can't remember, but you and I brainstormed different paths to making this a reality and came up with a few options. So far none of them have panned out. I can't even afford to buy the lot that's for sale."

Two splotches of pink mottled his cheeks. "What about crowdfunding?"

She pressed her lips into a thin line. *Patience. You need patience. The memory loss isn't his fault.* The silent mini pep talk didn't quell her racing pulse, though.

"We discussed crowdfunding as well. I'm anxious about asking people to kick in over a million dollars."

He looked thoughtful. "For the land and the facility?"

She nodded. "I've looked into partnering with groups who've generously supported community outreach in the past, corporations who can cover the costs, but the operating expenses are going to be incredibly high, so we'd have to require people to pay a membership fee. And even though Opportunity is part of a borough here, people are sensitive to fees and services and stretching their wallets."

"What if you posted on social media and asked

for support from people worldwide?" Max asked. "Surely there are countless humans across the nation or in other countries who want to help kids play sports?"

"Thanks for the suggestion." She tried to keep the irritation from creeping in. They'd been over that too. Several times.

"Will you tell me more about your motivation to do this?"

"My older brother Wyatt is a talented hockey player, and my parents always had to drive him a long way to play. But he was really sick when he was younger, Guillaume-Barré. It's a scary and debilitating condition. If it weren't for a brilliant pediatrician in Anchorage, I'm not sure Wyatt would've recovered. He was partially paralyzed, had to use supplemental oxygen and missed a ton of school." She shuttered at the memories. "Physical activity was the thing that helped him recover from his illness. He slowly started to get well, and eventually he was able to be physically active again. So to me, sports are super important, but we're limited in our options here, even though the community is growing. The bitterly cold winter weather is still an obstacle in hockey."

"And it's not for everyone."

"We've never been able to have football because kids don't have any recreational teams to play on."

"Well, football isn't everything."

"Yeah, but kids here want to be like kids they

see in other places. Not every family is like mine and has the resources to haul their kids ninety minutes to Fairbanks or over a hundred miles to Anchorage."

"I get it," Max said. "Well, if anybody can make this happen, I'm sure you can find a way. Are you interested in revisiting being a couple for the Spring Fling?"

"Are you?"

"Somebody asked me about it today when I was leaving the physical therapy clinic."

She sighed. "Some people have asked me too."

"Might be fun."

She didn't want to hurt his feelings. Really, she didn't. But it was getting harder and harder to say no without being incredibly honest. And how could she tell him that he'd crushed her when he'd left? Yes, his father's infidelity had been a terrible blow, but part of her still felt like he'd coped by choosing a big adventure over his relationship with her.

He seemed to sense a subject change was in order. "I know it's a lot to ask, and I hate asking you for anything else, but would you be willing to come with me to pick up my mom from the airport in Anchorage? I don't have a license."

"Sure, as long as I'm not working. I'll have to make sure Juliet is okay watching Fiona."

"Right, of course." Max dragged his hand

through his hair. "If it's too much trouble, then I'll figure something else out. I can ask Levi or..."

She reached over and clasped his forearm with her hand. "It's no trouble. I just need to make some arrangements. When is her flight?"

He hesitated. "February 2 at 2:15."

Oh no. She whipped out her phone, then scrolled to the last text she'd received from Mr. Butler. "Your dad is scheduled to fly home the night before."

Max's face turned pale. "You and Juliet already warned me that wouldn't work."

Hayley drew a calming breath, and then pasted on an optimistic smile. "We're all adults here. We can figure out some arrangements that keep everyone happy. Let me text my family. Maybe she can get a hotel room or someone would be willing to let her stay with them while she's here."

"I can't ask you to do that."

She hesitated, her fingers hovering over her phone's keyboard, and shot him a look. "Max, your mother and father will need their own space, especially your mom. She will want to be with people who make her feel comfortable and welcome. This is going to be an emotional reunion."

And possibly super dramatic. Max's parents' contentious divorce was one area of his life that she hoped he never recalled. It had been so ugly—not to mention the driving force behind his decision to leave town.

***

This was all so overwhelming.

Max sighed, then dragged his hand across his stubbly jaw and surveyed the three cardboard boxes he'd slid over to the sofa in the guesthouse. The unfamiliar handwriting scrawled on the outside indicated the box contained books and photo albums. He hesitated. Did he really want to dive into his past like this? The thought of coming face-to-face with his memories made his stomach clench—his body's indicator that he might want to proceed with caution. Had the uninjured version of him been this cautious?

Maybe he should ask Hayley.

He smiled. Man, she was a spunky thing. And she seemed to be knowledgeable about his life in Opportunity before he'd left. Was that how it would be with everyone he encountered in Opportunity? He'd only been here for a short time, but he wasn't sure. They knew him and his history in the small town, while he struggled to recall even the tiniest of relevant details. More doubt and unease washed over him. Maybe trying to recapture his memories wasn't the best idea after all.

Except when thoughts of his conversation with Hayley last night resurfaced, something bothered him. He'd sensed he'd pushed a little too far, or maybe just annoyed her when he'd gone back to the house last night to watch football and hang out. Yeah, okay. So it was a little weird how he showed up asking for some companionship. But he craved human interaction, and it felt weird staying out here by himself. Plus, as much as Hayley didn't seem to appreciate the facts when he pointed them out, Fiona did calm down when he held her.

At least he'd done one thing right. Comforting a cranky infant had to win him a few points with Hayley and prove he could help take care of the baby.

He reached over to peel back the tape on the nearest box when the phone rang. Hayley had mentioned the guesthouse had a separate landline, but who would call him here? Then again, news did travel fast in a small town. Maybe whoever was calling could help him out in some way. Besides, he gained nothing by ignoring the call.

Reluctantly, he crossed to the kitchen counter and answered the cordless phone. "Hello?"

"Max? Is that you?"

Max's scalp prickled. "This is Max. May I ask who's calling?"

"You don't recognize my voice? It's Dad. Why haven't you called?" The man's voice did sound strained. Almost worried.

Guilt twisted his insides. He shouldn't have procrastinated. "I'm... I'm back in Opportunity."

"Yes, I'm aware. Your mother reached out this morning to talk to me."

Max let out a sigh. "Look, I'm sorry I didn't

call sooner. The trip from Peru was exhausting, and I'm still trying to get my bearings. Memory loss makes everything harder."

Oh, brother. That sounded pathetic. How could he explain the almost constant feeling of being disoriented to his father without disappointing him? And why did he have an innate worry about disappointing this man he didn't remember?

There was a tense pause before his father spoke again. "It's been two years, Max. We've all been worried sick."

Max palmed the back of his neck. Was his father trying to make him feel guilty? He hadn't chosen to lose his memory or get stranded in a foreign country.

"I don't know what to say to that, honestly. It's not like I fell off that mountain on purpose. I only just pieced together enough information to figure out who I am, and it's going to take time for me to put my life back together."

"Understood." An awkward pause filled the connection. Then his father cleared his throat. "It was quite generous of Hayley and Juliet to take you in. Are you getting settled?"

He eyed the boxes at his feet. "Mostly."

"Good. I'm glad to hear that. Rachel and I look forward to reconnecting. I'll be back in Opportunity after my next trip to Paris."

"Great."

"I'll be in touch. Take care, son."

The line went dead.

Max pulled the phone away from his ear and stared at it. "So that was awkward."

Confusion churned his insides. Max set the phone on the counter. Had their relationship always been this strained?

Standing there feeling sorry for himself wouldn't change anything. Maybe he'd find more information if he started unpacking some of this stuff. He crossed the small room. Slowly, he peeled back the tape on the top of the closest cardboard box. Once he tugged back the flaps, true to the label, he found paperbacks and hardcover books. Fiction, mostly. He must have really liked this author. There were six written by the same guy. He glanced at the cover descriptions. All offered the same basic premise: a detective on a quest to solve a crime and reinstate justice. Max set them aside.

At the bottom of the box, he found a large envelope and a photo album. He lifted both out. Inside the envelope, he found rough sketches of a building, along with measurements and a few cryptic notes in unfamiliar handwriting. Huh. No clue what that was about. He set the envelope on the floor.

Next, Max ran his hand over the album's faux leather cover. "Here we go," he whispered.

He opened it. Photographs of him and guys he didn't recognize filled the first few pages. They'd evidently gone on various camping trips, and climbed a mountain he couldn't name. Max flipped through the plastic-coated pages. The old version of him had spent a ton of time outdoors. At least that part of him had remained consistent. He hadn't just been into climbing, either. Based on these photos, he'd also gone on white water rafting, hunting and fishing trips.

He flipped the pages. More photos of mountain climbing. He scanned a few of the captions with printed names, dates and Alaskan locations. Nothing tugged at his memory. What a shame. It looked like he'd had fun. He leafed to the back of that album and was about to close it when a picture of him and Hayley slipped out. His breath hitched. He picked up the photo and studied it. They were standing inside a building. A restaurant, maybe? Was this Jill's restaurant? He couldn't tell. He turned it over. Bummer. Nothing was written on the back.

He propped the photo against a tall candle in the middle of the side table. He'd have to ask her about it. He closed the album and set it on the table next to the candle. What if he kept looking at photos from his past? Would that spark any meaningful memories? He sat on the floor, surveyed his surroundings and then waited.

Nothing.

How had he lived a whole life that his brain had just discarded? It was like someone had dragged all the critical files into the recycle bin and emptied it. Frustrated, Max went to return the books to the box. A white paper napkin sat at the bottom. Huh. Must've missed that. He pulled it out. Another rudimentary sketch of a building filled the rectangle, along with neat cursive handwriting, and stick figure people playing ball. Clever. This looked similar to the drawings tucked inside the envelope. Was this connected to Hayley's plans for a rec center?

Max closed the cardboard flaps and pushed the box back next to the others. Then he stood and grabbed his jacket. Hesitating, he stared at the envelope. Would anything he'd found today help release his neurological logjam? Couldn't hurt to try. He tucked the photograph inside the envelope along with the napkin and headed for the door. Levi had offered to drive him to his appointment today, so he had taken him up on the kind gesture. With the mementos in hand, he headed for the house where he planned to ask Juliet some key questions. She was a little bit more open than her sister. Maybe she'd be able to shed some light on the details of the photo and the drawings.

If not, he'd be sure to ask Hayley when he saw her at the clinic because he was bound and determined to figure out how they'd been connected in the past. Even though he didn't remember, he sensed there was more than what she was letting on.

Chapter Five

She had to keep him busy. Focused. So determined to complete his physical therapy exercises that he wouldn't have time to ask any questions about his past.

Hayley rolled her mobile workstation across the clinic's linoleum floor to the cardio area where Max warmed up on a stationary bike. His leg muscles flexed as he peddled. She noted how his gray T-shirt stretched taut across his broad shoulders before quickly averting her gaze. This wasn't the time. Besides, her feelings for Max needed to stay where they belonged—locked away in the past.

Max glanced up at her and smiled. "Good morning. Nick told me to go ahead and get started warming up. I've ridden for seven minutes already."

"Great," Hayley said. "He's our PT aide. I asked him to get you started because my last patient required some extra time and attention. Thanks for your patience."

"Not a problem." His eyes sparkled as he held

her gaze. She couldn't look away. "I'm here and ready to work hard."

"That's a great attitude. Good for you." She offered a polite smile and then opened his electronic chart. Max kept peddling and she updated the notes, then double-checked the exercise plan she'd mapped out. Garrett had approved it, agreeing that they needed to work on reducing Max's swelling, improving his range of motion and making sure he stayed pain-free.

"Can I ask you a question?"

She slanted him a look. "As long as you keep peddling until your warm-up is finished."

"Have you talked to my dad lately?" Max swiped his upper arm across his forehead, quickly dabbing away the sweat dotting his skin.

Hayley shook her head. "Juliet and I usually text him with updates, and occasionally send a picture of Fiona. To be honest, he doesn't require a lot of information from us. I hope he's staying focused on his work and making sure Rachel receives the care she needs to get well."

Max's features shuttered. He didn't respond.

Had she said too much? Or said the wrong thing? "Have you heard from him?"

"Yeah, he called the landline in the guesthouse last night."

She stopped typing and waited for him to continue. "How did that go?"

Max shrugged one shoulder. "Not great. He

seemed annoyed that I hadn't reached out yet, and didn't really understand how difficult it's been for me to get back here."

"Your father is a very driven man. Maybe that's why he's been so successful."

Max's expression tightened.

Hayley nudged her workstation aside and joined him beside the bike. "Are you in pain?"

"My ankle doesn't hurt, if that's what you're asking. I'm mainly confused about what you're saying. My dad might be a great pilot, but he must not have been a very good husband."

Oh, boy. She did not want to get into all of that. Not now. She had to get him back on track. "Max, one of the questions we ask our new patients is what their goals are for this treatment. So what would you say your goals are?"

She paused, her fingers hovering over her keyboard.

A muscle in his jaw flexed. "If you're trying to protect me, you don't have to, Hayley. I know I said I wanted to hear only bits of information at a time, but I need to know about my past."

"I'm sure you do, but I'm not the one to tell you about your family's issues. My role here is to help you get well and take care of Fiona. That's it. What are your goals for physical therapy?"

"I want to regain my memory, obviously."

Right. She hesitated. "I was thinking more in

terms of your ankle, because that's what I'm treating."

"Oh." Two spots of color highlighted his cheekbones. "Then, my goals are that I want to be able to walk without limping and eventually jog. In exchange for my treatment, I want to be able to work on the renovation like I promised Garrett." He palmed the top of his head and stared out the window. A portion of Denali had emerged from the clouds, brilliant white against a blue-sky backdrop.

Hayley followed his gaze. Her stomach clenched, already anticipating what he was about to say.

"And I want to climb that mountain."

Her breath hitched.

He shot her a look. Hurt flashed in his eyes. "Why are you gasping? Is there something wrong with my goal?"

"I didn't gasp."

"You most certainly did." The bike beeped, indicating his warm-up was finished. He swung himself off it, towering over her. The aroma of his soap, mingled with the laundry soap they used at the house, enveloped her. She returned to her computer, eager to get him started on his first set of exercises.

"There are photos in albums that are mostly just me outdoors," Max said. "Climbing must've been a big part of who I was. Maybe who I still am."

Her palms turned clammy. "Let's start with the

gentle stretching exercises to increase range of motion. Remember? I showed you how to do this at the house."

Nodding, Max took the white towel she handed him. "Why do I get the sense that maybe you're not thrilled about this?"

"Stretching?"

He shook his head. "Climbing."

Hayley clamped her mouth closed. Once she input the information, she forced herself to meet his gaze.

"Because climbing is how we lost you," she said softly. "Denali is extremely dangerous. It comes at a big cost, that's all. I'm just surprised you're ready to get back out there."

He cocked his head to one side. "Were you and I close? I mean, before?"

Now it was her turn to blush. "We talked a lot. You always sat in my section at the Sluice Box."

"How often?"

"At least once a week."

"Was I nice to you?"

She couldn't stop her smile. "Of course, Max. You're nice to everyone. At first you were aloof, sort of gruff. But I noticed you played a game of tag outside with the kids waiting for a table in the restaurant. Then I saw you give rides to tourists who didn't want to walk back to the hotel after dinner, and I knew—"

"Hey, there he is." Garrett joined them in the

exercise area, and clapped Max gently on the shoulder. "How's it going?"

Hayley blew out a relieved breath. She'd never been so happy to have her manager interrupt a conversation.

"I'm doing well, thanks." Max stretched the towel in a U-shape around his ankle then tugged both ends toward his body, pulling his toes toward the ceiling. Hayley watched from her safe vantage point behind her laptop. At least he followed instructions.

"Do you have any updates on your building plans?" Max tipped his head toward the crowded patient treatment area. "I see what you mean about needing some more space."

Garrett linked his arms across his chest. "One hundred percent. I'm so ready for spring. We can blow out that wall and add on about five hundred square feet."

"Wait," Hayley interrupted. "You're going to take down a wall? I thought you were joking about that part."

Garrett smiled. "Don't worry. There won't be any delays or disruptions in patient care. Not quite sure how the new addition will take shape. That's the project manager's responsibility."

"Noted." She went back to updating Max's progress in the electronic chart while he chatted about building plans, supplies and timelines.

She only half listened, though. Deeply distracted by how close she had come to letting Max know how she'd really felt about him.

Why hadn't he regained any memories yet?

Closing his eyes, Max gritted his teeth and tipped his head back against the sofa cushions. Trying to recall a specific memory of his life in Opportunity before he left for Peru was like wandering down a long hallway and jiggling locked doorknobs over and over. Nothing budged. His chest tightened. He'd been here for a week. Why hadn't coming home helped him heal?

He swallowed a frustrated groan. What if he never remembered? What if he lived the rest of his life with only the new memories he'd created since his accident?

Lord, please. Help me remember. This isn't fair.

Max opened his eyes, grabbed a throw pillow with both hands and squeezed it as tight as he could.

Hayley looked up from where she sat in the recliner, working on her laptop. "Are you all right?"

He glanced at Fiona asleep in the bouncy, vibrating chair on the living floor between them.

"Yeah," he said, gesturing to the plastic bags of ice on his ankle. "When I'm icing, I try to concentrate and recall memories, but my brain is not cooperating. Sometimes I get super frustrated, and now I'm worried that I'll never remember."

He didn't want to complain, but she did ask.

And selfishly, he was starting to wonder if she held the key to unlocking some of those doors. But when it came to getting more information out of her, she clammed up. What was it about his past that she wasn't interested in discussing? The ice shifted in the plastic bag, and he leaned forward to adjust it. He'd set a timer on his watch, and he only had seven more minutes to go.

Hayley put her laptop aside. The compassion in her eyes somehow eased the pain that had lodged in his chest. "I'm truly sorry that you're going through this. I can't imagine how hard it must be to move back home yet feel like a stranger."

"Thank you." He set the pillow aside. "Before my father gets home and you leave for the party, I wanted to ask you about a photograph and some sketches I found. I showed them to Juliet, and we both wondered if it was your original plan for the recreational venue."

She frowned. "Sketches? Where did you find them?"

"In a box of my stuff in the guesthouse."

Outside, the crunch of snow under tires and the thrum of a vehicle in the driveway snagged his attention. "That's probably him, isn't it?"

She nodded.

A door slammed, followed by muffled footsteps on the porch. Then a key turned in the lock and the front door opened.

A tall middle-aged man stepped inside, towing

a roller bag behind him. He wore a black winter jacket, black dress pants and an expensive pair of shiny black lace-up shoes. His dark hair was cut short on the sides and slightly longer on top.

When his gaze landed on Max, the man's blue eyes welled. Then he scrubbed his hand over his clean-shaven face. Was he crying?

"Max." His voice broke and he spread his arms wide.

Max hesitated. This must be his father. Was he supposed to hug the guy? He shot Hayley a silent plea for help.

"Here, let me get those." Hayley stood up from the recliner and removed the ice bags from his ankle. She avoided eye contact but wore a guarded expression. One he'd learned to recognize just in the short time he'd been here. Beside them, Fiona kicked her feet and started to fuss.

"Max, this is your dad, Jack Butler." Hayley angled her body slightly toward the man and offered a polite smile. "Welcome home, Mr. Butler. Fiona is just waking up from her nap, so I'll take care of her and let you two get reacquainted."

Hayley scooped Fiona into her arms and quickly left the room. Max's mouth went dry. He forced himself to stay present. Even though he longed to follow Hayley to Fiona's nursery. These reunions were getting a smidge easier, but the way that his scalp prickled warned him that maybe he and his dad hadn't had the best relationship. He forced himself to move toward the man. Gave the standard awkward back slap paired with a perfunctory embrace.

"It's good to see you, son." Jack stepped back, his Adam's apple bobbing as he swallowed hard. He gripped Max's shoulders as his piercing eyes scanned Max's face. His father was a broad-shouldered man and looked physically fit. Max still had a good three to four inches in height over him. And he wasn't about to let the guy intimidate him. He didn't have any facts or photos to back up his feelings, but he'd learned to trust his gut reactions to the people he encountered who'd known him before his accident.

Max put some space between them. "How was your trip?"

"Long. Paris to LaGuardia, then an unexpected delay until I found seats on connecting flights into Anchorage." His father nudged his roller bag out of the way, then shrugged out of his jacket and hung it on a hook nearby. He wore a crisp white button-down and a tie.

"Huh. I thought maybe you'd stop over in California to see your wife."

"I'll see her again in a few days. She's busy trying to get well. Besides, I have to keep flying. Somebody's got to finance this lifestyle, you know." He swept his arm through the air, gesturing at the spacious living room with leather furniture and sophisticated electronics. Jack's too-white smile and his tanned skin provoked more questions about how his father spent his free time. He'd save those inquiries for later, though.

The sound of Fiona crying through the baby monitor caught his dad's attention. Jack moved quickly across the room and turned off the volume. "We probably don't want to listen to that, do we?"

Max cupped the back of his neck. "I've gotten used to it. She cries quite a bit."

"Yeah, I know. That's part of the problem. The crying is what made her mother so upset."

Max winced. That sounded difficult, and yet his father didn't seem sympathetic. Hopefully Hayley would come back downstairs soon or Juliet would pop in unexpectedly and give him a buffer. He so did not know what to say to this man.

"You want to go grab dinner?" Jack paused and flipped through a stack of mail sitting on the console table in the entryway. "Have you been back to the Sluice Box yet? It was always one of your favorite hangouts. I mean, probably because Hayley worked there."

"Oh?"

His dad studied him. "You don't remember? Wow, Max." His dad chuckled. "You really have forgotten all the important stuff. You and Hayley were—"

"Mr. Butler, would you like to hold Fiona?" Hayley strode back into the room and thrust the baby into his dad's arms. Fiona stopped crying and shoved two fingers in her mouth. His dad struggled to hold the baby.

"Um, sure. I'll hold her for a minute. Hey, Fiona." He tentatively patted her leg. "You've grown."

"She's doing great," Hayley said.

"Still cries a lot, I hear."

Hayley frowned. "I'm sure she misses you."

Jack shot her a dark look. "No, she cried almost constantly, even when my wife and I were both here."

"I'm going to clean up those ice bags and take care of a couple of chores. Then I'll be on my way," Hayley said.

"On your way? Where?" Jack frowned. "I just got here."

"Exactly." Hayley's thin smile barely contained her irritation. "You're here. That means I don't need to be. I told you that I'd be taking the evening off once you arrived."

"But Max and I are going to go grab dinner."

"Oh, how nice. Well, Fiona is portable. You can pop her infant car seat right into the base. It's still installed in the back of your car."

A vein bulged in the middle of his forehead. "Hayley, this is not what we discussed."

"It's absolutely what we discussed, sir. I sent you a text, remember? You responded yesterday. Told me you were more than happy to give me and Juliet the evening off to celebrate our father's birthday. Would you like me to empty the dishwasher before I go?"

"Hayley, we've got it," Max said quietly. "Go. Enjoy your family."

"Thanks. I hope you guys have a wonderful time." She squeezed his arm then turned and strolled into the kitchen.

"I'm... Is..." Dad glanced at Max. "Could you hold her for a second?"

"Sure." Max nestled the baby against his shoulder and patted her backside. "Are you hungry? Let's go fix your bottle."

He followed his dad into the kitchen where Hayley had just tucked her phone into her purse and grabbed her keys off the counter. There was no way he'd let him give Hayley a hard time. She and Juliet already had plans. They'd worked it all out. Max had agreed to stay with Fiona until Juliet came back at nine thirty. Why did his father feel the need to interfere?

"Wait. You were there when Max and his father saw each other for the first time?" Savannah asked as she unboxed birthday candles and set them on the counter.

Hayley hesitated, unsure if she should discuss these emotional reunions with others.

Before she could respond, laughter rippled into the Morgan family's cozy kitchen. Savannah, Juliet and Hayley stood around the island, prepping the cake and ice cream.

"How did that go?" Mom pulled two cartons of vanilla and chocolate ice cream from the side-by-side freezer. "I imagine Jack was overwhelmed."

"He got a little choked up," Hayley said. "Max looked...uncertain. It was a little tense, to be honest." She pulled her phone from her back pocket to check her text messages. Neither Jack nor Max had reached out. Yet.

"Are you checking to see if they're texting you?" Juliet asked. "I'll be over there by 9:30, I promise."

"I'm just a little worried." Hayley found the ice cream scoop in one of the drawers and handed it to her mother. "Jack wanted to take Max out to dinner, so of course, they'll take Fiona with them."

"Jack is Fiona's father." Savannah pried the lids off the ice cream cartons. "Surely he and Max can take care of her for a few hours. Besides, you said Max wanted to contribute and do his part, so this is his chance."

Hayley and Juliet exchanged doubtful looks. "Yeah, Jack's a super hands-off dad, though," Hayley said, putting her phone away. "He implied that Juliet and I needed to change our plans to accommodate him."

"I'm glad you didn't cave," Juliet said. "The man needs to spend some quality time with both of his children. By the way, when does Jack leave town again?"

"Usually, he's home for about a week, but he said he wants to visit Rachel again before his next trip. So if he can get on a standby flight out of Anchorage and back to California, he'll be gone sooner."

Juliet counted out clean forks and spoons. "Hopefully before Cindi gets here, right?"

An awkward silence blanketed the space.

"Max's mother is coming?" Savannah asked quietly.

Hayley nodded. "Tomorrow."

"You girls are doing a fabulous job with that precious baby," Mom said. She opened the kitchen drawer and pulled out a book of matches. "Let's get these candles on the cake."

A few minutes later, they all went into the dining room. Mom led the way, carrying the cake topped with two candles shaped like a six and a two. Savannah's husband, Levi, and their kids, Wren and Connor, sat at one end of the long farmhouse-style table. Wyatt, the oldest Morgan kid, sat beside their dad, while four of Dad's close friends occupied the opposite side.

Hayley tried her best to stay present as they set the cake on the table in front of their dad. His face lit up, and the lines at the corners of his eyes crinkled as he grinned and reached for Mom's hand. Hayley crowded in beside her sisters. Savannah draped her arm around Levi's shoulders.

Wyatt sat alone at the end of the table. He

didn't have a girlfriend right now, much to everyone's disappointment. Her older brother was such a good guy. Too bad he hadn't met someone to marry. Maybe his laser focus on hockey and his work didn't leave time for a relationship.

Or maybe he was just afraid.

She shoved that thought aside. Probably because it hit too close to home. Part of her wished Max was here. Although he did need to reconnect with his dad. Still, she'd gotten used to having him around and now she wanted more.

Hayley mumbled the last few lines of the birthday song, but her thoughts kept wandering to Max. Did he know how to take care of a baby in a restaurant?

"Make a wish, dear," Mom said. Dad kissed her knuckles, then took a deep breath and blew out all the candles.

"Yay!" Wren squealed, clapping her hands. Everyone else laughed and clapped too. Not that Hayley wasn't happy to be celebrating her father's birthday, but she was just so distracted. And probably wouldn't rest easy until Juliet got back to the Butlers' and confirmed that Fiona was fine.

"Hayley?"

Mom's voice tugged her back to reality. She quickly looked around the table. "What?"

All eyes were on her. Heat warmed her face.

Her parents' friend Sandy offered a polite smile.

"I was just asking how things are going with the Butlers."

Hayley shifted from one foot to the other. "About as well as can be expected."

"Does Max really have amnesia?" The woman leaned forward and rested her chin on her hands in a tell-me-everything pose.

"He really does." Hayley stepped closer to the table and cleared away the dinner plates to make room for dessert. "He can't remember a thing from before he hit his head in Peru."

"Don't that beat all, honey?" Sandy nudged her husband. "Have you ever heard of such a thing?"

The man shook his head. "Only in books and movies."

"It's more common than people realize," Hayley said.

"Oh?" The woman frowned. "Hasn't happened to anyone around here before."

"True." Hayley leaned over Wyatt's shoulder and then stacked his plate on top of the others in her hands. "Max might be the first in Opportunity to have accomplished something so noteworthy." She followed her mother and Savannah back into the kitchen and slid the stack of plates onto the counter beside the sink.

"What's wrong, dear?"

"Sandy is being a busybody," she whispered. "Why can't people just leave Max alone?"

Her mother and Savannah exchanged glances.

"What? What am I missing?"

"You're getting a little defensive, dear." Mom slid a sympathetic glance her way. "I think people are just naturally curious. I mean, after all, we thought he was gone forever, and now he's back."

"Plus, all his memories from when he lived here are gone. It's quite a story," Savannah said.

Hayley leaned against the counter and crossed her arms over her chest. "Do you think it's not true?"

"That's not what I said." Savannah plated a slice of cake, then added a scoop of vanilla ice cream. "People are prone to talk about each other. That's all."

A notification pinged on Hayley's phone. She checked it to see a message in her DMs from Weston. She thumbed away the notification. So not who she wanted to hear from right now.

Savannah's gaze found hers. "Everything okay?"

Hayley nodded, then looked away.

Mom hesitated, studying her. "Do you want your kids to have cake and ice cream, Savannah?"

"A small slice for Wren, please, with a tiny bit of vanilla ice cream. I'll let the baby taste my ice cream," Savannah said.

"Got it." Mom plated another slice of cake.

"I don't see how gossiping will help Max recover from his head trauma. If people really cared, maybe they could find more productive ways to help," Hayley continued. "That's why I'm hesitant to serve on the Spring Fling court. People are just going to use it as an excuse to stare at him and ask more nosy questions."

"Maybe instead of focusing on the negative aspects of people's curiosity, you can use Spring Fling to remind people that you still have a big dream to make Opportunity a better place. For everyone." Savannah slid a couple plates of dessert across the counter. "Don't worry. Max can hold his own."

"I'll deliver these." Hayley picked up two plates of dessert and carried them into the dining room. Savannah's encouraging words did little to buoy her attitude. Because making her dream a reality—not to mention guarding her heart—seemed next to impossible right now.

Chapter Six

This was a terrible idea. He should've asked his mother to reschedule.

"What if I see her and I don't feel any connection?" Max asked as they waited outside the security checkpoint at the Anchorage airport. He was clutching a bouquet of grocery store flowers in his sweaty hand. He looked at the picture on his new phone one more time. Mom had texted him the photo yesterday, and Juliet and Hayley had both confirmed that she was in fact his mother.

And in about five minutes, they'd be reunited.

If only he had memories of her.

"She wants to see you," Hayley said, her gentle tone softening the sharp edges of his anxiety. "You're her only son. Imagine how she must feel, living for two years without you. Then hearing you're actually alive, but she has to travel thousands of miles to see you again. How do—"

"All right, all right." Max held up his palm. "You've made your point. I'm just…nervous."

Hayley's eyes filled with compassion. "I see that. You can do this, Max."

Her kindness was a magnet, drawing him in and making him wonder—again—if they'd been more than friends. But this wasn't the time to think about his feelings for Hayley. So he turned away. Forced himself to focus on the passengers strolling toward the security checkpoint. None of the women resembled the photo on his phone.

Frankly, he didn't relish the thought of another tear-filled interaction, complete with awkward hugs and shocked expressions. Why couldn't he remember the people he'd once cared about most?

When he concentrated hard and tried to think about his mom, his stubborn brain only served up images from the photo albums he'd flipped through countless times.

Hayley and Juliet had tried to fill in some of the blanks. They'd said things like "she has a great laugh" and "a beautiful smile." He assumed from looking at the most recent picture that she had taken good care of herself. Based on the freckles sprinkled across her cheeks and her tanned arms, she probably liked being outside. And he appreciated that she'd dropped everything and hopped on a plane to come see him. But man, he was so nervous.

What would they talk about? What if he didn't feel a sense of connection? What if he hurt her feelings with all the things about their shared history that he couldn't recall? A knot tightened in his gut. This was so hard.

People streamed past them, and then he saw a woman jogging toward him with tears streaming down her face and her arms stretched out.

"Max." She breathed out his name, then clapped a hand over her mouth. She dropped her bag at her feet. "Can I hug you?"

"Hi. Yeah, sure. Absolutely." He laughed nervously and let her hug him. The strength of her embrace and the way her body trembled as she squeezed him tight, crying softly, brought an unexpected ball of emotion to his throat. So he wasn't totally devoid of feelings. That had to count for something, right? He swallowed hard, then patted her on the back.

When she pulled away, he offered a smile. "You must be my mom."

"Yes. The one and only." She sniffed. "Let me look at you."

She scanned him from the top of his head to the tips of his toes before meeting his gaze again. "I'm so sorry." She swiped at the moisture on her cheeks. "You probably hate that I'm making such a scene."

His chest tightened. "You don't have to be sorry. It's all right."

"I really thought we'd lost you forever, honey."

"Well, here I am." He held out the bouquet of daisies and yellow roses—another thing Juliet and

Hayley had helped him with. The plastic crinkled. "These are for you."

She glanced down at the bouquet and splayed her hand across her chest. Fresh tears welled in her blue eyes. "You didn't have to do that."

"Of course I did. You're my mom, and you came all this way to see me. It's the least I could do."

She cradled the bouquet in her arms, then gave Hayley a wobbly smile. "Hi, Hayley. It's good to see you again."

Hayley stepped closer and offered a side hug. "It's nice to see you too, Mrs. B." Then she sucked in a breath. Her cheeks turned red. "I'm so sorry. You probably don't—"

"I didn't change my name," Mom said. "But feel free to call me Cindi. I know there's a new Mrs. Butler now."

An awkward silence hung between them, and Max hid a wince. He cleared his throat and said, "Let's talk while we go and get your suitcase." He hoisted her backpack over his shoulder. "Unless this is all you brought?"

"I checked one bag." She led the way like she'd walked this route many times before. Of course she had.

"How was your flight?" He sidestepped a couple racing down the corridor.

"The first one from Bozeman to Seattle was fine, and then I had a layover, then another flight here. Both were good. I watched a couple of movies and enjoyed some good food. I was just so anxious to get here, though, that I haven't really slept much the last few days."

"You can take a nap while Hayley drives us back to Opportunity. Unless there's something here in Anchorage you want to do first."

She hesitated. "We should probably visit your grandparents. Are you up for that?"

"Sure. Where do they live?"

"Not too far from here. It's on the way. So I guess if you're asking, then you haven't seen them?"

"I wanted to see you first."

She frowned. "You really don't remember your grandparents?"

"No. I'm sorry, I don't." He paused at the top of the escalator and let Hayley and his mother go first. "Hayley's doing the best she can to fill in the gaps for me, though."

"Oh, my." Mom gripped the handrail, then spoke over her shoulder as they glided down toward baggage claim. "Well, your grandfather probably won't say a whole lot, and your grandmother will ask a dozen questions."

"I'm getting used to the questions part. People in Opportunity are a curious bunch."

She laughed. "True."

They made small talk while they waited for her bag, then made their way to the parking lot.

Max opened the back hatch of Hayley's vehicle and slid his mother's bags inside.

"Hope I'm not keeping you two from anything," Cindi said. "Hayley, are you sure you have time to stop and visit my parents?"

Hayley hesitated. "We have time to visit for about an hour."

Max closed the hatch. "Is Juliet okay with that?"

Hayley pulled her phone from her purse. "I'll text her to double-check."

Mom stood on the car's passenger side, her brow furrowed. "What am I missing?"

Oh boy. Max raked his hand through his hair. "Juliet and Hayley are working for Dad."

"I see. Doing what, exactly?" Mom's words were clipped.

Hayley shot Max a panicked look.

"Nannying." Max climbed in the back seat. "Hayley and Juliet are splitting the duties, and I'm filling in wherever I can."

"Oh." His mother pressed her lips into a flat line. She stood outside the car, with one hand on the frame of the open door.

Hayley slid behind the wheel but said nothing. Tension snaked through the cab. Max leaned between the gap in the front row seats. "Mom, is this going to be a problem?"

"Is what going to be a problem?"

"That Hayley works for him, and I live in his guesthouse?"

"No, of course not." Mom eased onto the passenger seat, then closed the door. She reached for her seat belt. "A little heads-up would've been nice, that's all."

"I'm sorry. I didn't mean to upset you. Again, I don't remember any details about the past. So if there are things you need me to know, you're just going to have to fill in the holes."

She twisted in her seat. Her mouth dropped open. She looked like he'd stomped on her pinky toe.

He stifled a groan. "What? What did I say?"

"You have no idea why your father and I got divorced?"

"Nope."

Her lower lip trembled. "I—I can't believe it's not obvious."

Oh no. He reached for her hand. "Can we focus on reconnecting, please?"

She swiped at her tears with her sleeve, then placed her hand in his. "Yes."

"Okay. Well, I can't remember you right now, but my memory loss doesn't change our relationship. We might just have to get to know each other again. Are you okay with that?"

She nodded.

"So that means you're going to have to tell me things that you want me to know."

She tugged her hand free and finished buckling her seat belt. "Honestly, there's probably a lot of things you don't need to know."

nger and healthier every day. Her care team
ntioned discharging her early."
An incoming text message caught her attention.

there. Just following up on our last conversa-
n about Spring Fling. Are you and Max still sit-
g this one out, or can I nominate you for the
yal court? No pressure or anything, but we just
d a couple drop out.

"Oh, boy." Hayley held her phone out so Max
uld see the screen. "This is from Jill. Last call
volunteer for the Spring Fling royal court."
His gaze pinged between her and the phone.
A mischievous grin tipped up the corners of his
mouth. "I'm in. You?"

Savannah's words from the night before echoed
n her head. Maybe her sister was right. Maybe
she needed to shift her focus. What if serving her
community ended up moving her one step closer
to her achieving her goal?

"Fine. I'll do it." She quickly sent a message
back to Jill confirming they'd both serve, then put
her phone down and scooped up the grocery bags.

"Don't sound so thrilled." Max followed her
into the kitchen.

"Maybe I'm overthinking things. Who knows.
It might end up being really fun." Hayley formed
her mouth into what she hoped was a convincing
smile, then stacked some oatmeal and bananas on

Oh, brother. He slumped back in his seat as
Hayley started the engine. *Lord, give me patience. Please.*

Why couldn't people just fill in the gaps for him? Had he been a terrible person? What was his mother trying to protect him from? Somehow, he had to dig deep and find the truth. Because it wasn't just the little things. Icy dread settled in his core. There was something they weren't telling him. And he wouldn't rest until he figured it out.

"Oh, no. This can't be happening."

Hayley scanned the text messages from Jack Butler on her phone and then shoved the device in her pocket without responding. There were no words. Max was not equipped to handle this. She snagged the grocery bags from the back seat of the car, as her phone pinged with another incoming message. She ignored it and nudged the car door closed with her hip. Shivering, she hurried toward the house. Snowflakes drifted down from the gray sky, finding the open space inside her jacket collar at the base of her neck. Shivering, she clomped up the steps, set the grocery bags down, then opened the door.

"Max, are you here?"

"Hey, look," Max said. "Fiona just smiled at me."

Hayley set the bags of groceries on the floor before going to find Max. He sat on the couch in the living room, an empty bottle on the coffee table. He had Fiona nestled in the crook of his arm. She cooed and stared up at him.

Seriously? She never smiles at me. She promptly batted back the petty thought.

"Maybe it's just gas."

"Ha." Max eyed the bags at her feet. "Are there more groceries in the car?"

"No, this is all I brought. I do have some news, though." She hung up her jacket and took a deep breath.

"What's up?"

"Remember how we already had plans to invite your mom for dinner tonight?"

"Yeah. She's still coming, right?"

"Yep. And guess who else is less than an hour away?"

All the color drained from his face. "My dad and Rachel."

"Not Rachel. Your dad's on his way, though. Mechanical failure with his plane, so his flight's canceled. He's going to go out again tomorrow."

"Oh, boy." Max gently shifted Fiona to his other arm. "This sounds complicated."

"I do have some good news." Hayley took off her boots and left them in the entryway. "Juliet will bring your mom over in a few minutes, and I—we—have plenty of food here. Thanks to my parents, who let me pilfer from their freezer. We'll have a scrumptious meal. My mom's homemade spaghetti sauce is to die for, by th[e] salad, French bread and I grabbed ice cream from the store on my wa[y]

"That does sound amazing. But ing great about this. Can they even a meal together?"

"Good question. I hope so. Hey, ca[n] ate that smile?" Hayley pulled her ph[one] back pocket. "I want to take a picture

"Maybe." Max made a silly face some gibberish to Fiona. She cooed, her legs. Sure enough. Her little mo[uth] into a toothless smile. "Oh, wow," H[ayley] "She's adorable."

They tried to re-create the mome[nt] Fiona was a little less interested in part

"There." Hayley snapped several photos, up her phone to show Max.

His brow furrowed. "Sort of. Her fir[st] was better, but I'm sure there'll be more.

Hayley chose the best image, attache[d] text message for Rachel, then sent it off quick note explaining that they'd tried to Fiona smiling at Max.

"How's Rachel doing?" Max gently s[hifted] Fiona onto his shoulder and patted her back. ceiving that picture won't upset her, will it?

Hayley hesitated. "I don't think so. We sen[d] frequent updates, and your dad says she's ge[tting]

the counter, folded the grocery bag and stowed it in the pantry.

"What did you mean about Rachel's discharge? How early is early?"

"I'm really not sure. Maybe your dad will have a specific date?"

Boy, it still irritated her that Fiona had smiled for Max.

She pushed the annoyance down as she finished emptying the bags and arranging the groceries they needed for dinner. How had Fiona's preference for Max sidelined her emotionally?

Don't be petty. She placed the last of the items in the cupboard. As she closed the door and turned away, Max spoke quietly to Fiona.

"Hey, little one." His smooth voice turned Hayley's insides to mush. Warmth bloomed in her chest.

Fiona cooed, drawing another smile from Max. Hayley couldn't help but stare at the curve of his angular jaw. Or the lines that crinkled at the corners of his eyes. More conflicting emotions washed over her. She couldn't deny the jealousy. It had taken root like a noxious weed, snaking through her insides, and threatening to choke out her joy. But it was quickly being overshadowed by something else. Something she really didn't want to fully acknowledge.

Seeing Max cradle his infant half sister with such tenderness brought her old feelings for him rushing back. Turning away, she grabbed a canister of sanitizing wipes from under the kitchen sink and went to work scrubbing at a stubborn spot on the countertop. She tried pushing her conflicting emotions away, burying them down deep where they couldn't cause trouble.

Except she couldn't resist stealing another glance at Max holding Fiona. Then he started singing. Fiona stared at him. Captivated. Their undeniable bond provoked another pang of longing. She shook her head, desperate to dispel the thoughts threatening to overwhelm her. Max couldn't know how she truly felt about him.

She wiped down the counter with more force than necessary. There had to be a way to distract herself from the ache settling in her chest. And the surge of guilt for hiding her feelings from him.

What if she told him exactly what had happened between them?

No.

She couldn't let him see the turmoil brewing. Swallowing hard, she tossed the wipe in the trash then softly approached Max and Fiona. The baby's eyes drooped as she drifted off to sleep.

Max carefully stood and carried her to the Moses basket sitting on the floor nearby. He placed her on the thin cushion. Hayley held her breath. Fiona almost always woke up as soon as she realized no one was holding her.

Max backed away slowly. When he turned

Oh, brother. He slumped back in his seat as Hayley started the engine. *Lord, give me patience. Please.*

Why couldn't people just fill in the gaps for him? Had he been a terrible person? What was his mother trying to protect him from? Somehow, he had to dig deep and find the truth. Because it wasn't just the little things. Icy dread settled in his core. There was something they weren't telling him. And he wouldn't rest until he figured it out.

"Oh, no. This can't be happening."

Hayley scanned the text messages from Jack Butler on her phone and then shoved the device in her pocket without responding. There were no words. Max was not equipped to handle this. She snagged the grocery bags from the back seat of the car, as her phone pinged with another incoming message. She ignored it and nudged the car door closed with her hip. Shivering, she hurried toward the house. Snowflakes drifted down from the gray sky, finding the open space inside her jacket collar at the base of her neck. Shivering, she clomped up the steps, set the grocery bags down, then opened the door.

"Max, are you here?"

"Hey, look," Max said. "Fiona just smiled at me."

Hayley set the bags of groceries on the floor before going to find Max. He sat on the couch in the living room, an empty bottle on the coffee table. He had Fiona nestled in the crook of his arm. She cooed and stared up at him.

Seriously? She never smiles at me. She promptly batted back the petty thought.

"Maybe it's just gas."

"Ha." Max eyed the bags at her feet. "Are there more groceries in the car?"

"No, this is all I brought. I do have some news, though." She hung up her jacket and took a deep breath.

"What's up?"

"Remember how we already had plans to invite your mom for dinner tonight?"

"Yeah. She's still coming, right?"

"Yep. And guess who else is less than an hour away?"

All the color drained from his face. "My dad and Rachel."

"Not Rachel. Your dad's on his way, though. Mechanical failure with his plane, so his flight's canceled. He's going to go out again tomorrow."

"Oh, boy." Max gently shifted Fiona to his other arm. "This sounds complicated."

"I do have some good news." Hayley took off her boots and left them in the entryway. "Juliet will bring your mom over in a few minutes, and I—we—have plenty of food here. Thanks to my parents, who let me pilfer from their freezer. We'll have a scrumptious meal. My mom's homemade spaghetti sauce is to die for, by the way. There's salad, French bread and I grabbed brownies and ice cream from the store on my way home."

"That does sound amazing. But I'm not feeling great about this. Can they even handle eating a meal together?"

"Good question. I hope so. Hey, can you re-create that smile?" Hayley pulled her phone from her back pocket. "I want to take a picture for Rachel."

"Maybe." Max made a silly face and spoke some gibberish to Fiona. She cooed, then kicked her legs. Sure enough. Her little mouth curved into a toothless smile. "Oh, wow," Hayley said. "She's adorable."

They tried to re-create the moment again. Fiona was a little less interested in participating. "There." Hayley snapped several photos, then held up her phone to show Max.

His brow furrowed. "Sort of. Her first smile was better, but I'm sure there'll be more."

Hayley chose the best image, attached it to a text message for Rachel, then sent it off with a quick note explaining that they'd tried to capture Fiona smiling at Max.

"How's Rachel doing?" Max gently shifted Fiona onto his shoulder and patted her back. "Receiving that picture won't upset her, will it?"

Hayley hesitated. "I don't think so. We send her frequent updates, and your dad says she's getting stronger and healthier every day. Her care team mentioned discharging her early."

An incoming text message caught her attention.

Hi there. Just following up on our last conversation about Spring Fling. Are you and Max still sitting this one out, or can I nominate you for the royal court? No pressure or anything, but we just had a couple drop out.

"Oh, boy." Hayley held her phone out so Max could see the screen. "This is from Jill. Last call to volunteer for the Spring Fling royal court."

His gaze pinged between her and the phone. A mischievous grin tipped up the corners of his mouth. "I'm in. You?"

Savannah's words from the night before echoed in her head. Maybe her sister was right. Maybe she needed to shift her focus. What if serving her community ended up moving her one step closer to her achieving her goal?

"Fine. I'll do it." She quickly sent a message back to Jill confirming they'd both serve, then put her phone down and scooped up the grocery bags.

"Don't sound so thrilled." Max followed her into the kitchen.

"Maybe I'm overthinking things. Who knows. It might end up being really fun." Hayley formed her mouth into what she hoped was a convincing smile, then stacked some oatmeal and bananas on around, he caught Hayley's gaze. Silence hung between them, loaded with unspoken words and her buried feelings. Max moved closer, his expression unreadable. With every step he took toward her, Hayley's pulse sped. She took a step back, trying to maintain a safe distance, but she bumped up against the kitchen counter.

Max's gaze, intense and unwavering, locked on hers. Could he see right through her? Right through her carefully constructed facade and straight to the truth she'd tried so hard to conceal?

"Hayley," Max said, his voice low and full of emotion. "There's something I need to tell you."

She gripped the counter's edge with both hands. A million thoughts swirled through her head. What was he going to say? He took another step closer, erasing the gap between them. She held her breath and waited for his words.

His gaze drifted toward her lips, then slowly roamed her face. Uncertainty flickered in his eyes. Neither of them spoke. What was he thinking?

"I know things are about to get messy," he said softly. "No matter what happens tonight between my father and mother, I want you to know that having you here, helping me navigate this, means a lot."

Another rush of conflicting emotions flooded through her. She swallowed hard. Was he trying to make her melt? The spicy scent of his aftershave enveloped her. Clouded her judgment. It would be so easy to tell him how much he'd meant to her. How often she'd dreamed of a future that included the two of them navigating life's peaks and valleys together. Forever.

The front door opened.

Max cleared his throat, looking slightly flustered, then stepped back. "We should intercept them before they wake Fiona."

Hayley nodded, grateful for the distraction. They both left the kitchen, leaving behind the charged atmosphere that lingered between them. She'd almost kissed him.

As Max quietly welcomed his mom and Juliet, Hayley couldn't shake off the weight of Max's tender words. His vulnerable comment provoked her. Left her feeling both elated and anxious.

A notification pinged on her phone. She pulled it from her back pocket and checked the screen. Weston had commented on a recent selfie she'd posted.

Looking good, girl. Let's talk soon.

Her stomach tightened. Talk about *what*?

She put her phone away without responding then greeted her sister and Max's mom. "Hi there."

"Hi." Juliet's keen eyes darted between Hayley and Max. Hayley silently pleaded with her not to say a word. Juliet flashed a knowing smile be-around, he caught Hayley's gaze. Silence hung between them, loaded with unspoken words and her buried feelings. Max moved closer, his expression unreadable. With every step he took toward her, Hayley's pulse sped. She took a step back, trying to maintain a safe distance, but she bumped up against the kitchen counter.

Max's gaze, intense and unwavering, locked on hers. Could he see right through her? Right through her carefully constructed facade and straight to the truth she'd tried so hard to conceal?

"Hayley," Max said, his voice low and full of emotion. "There's something I need to tell you."

She gripped the counter's edge with both hands. A million thoughts swirled through her head. What was he going to say? He took another step closer, erasing the gap between them. She held her breath and waited for his words.

His gaze drifted toward her lips, then slowly roamed her face. Uncertainty flickered in his eyes. Neither of them spoke. What was he thinking?

"I know things are about to get messy," he said softly. "No matter what happens tonight between my father and mother, I want you to know that having you here, helping me navigate this, means a lot."

Another rush of conflicting emotions flooded through her. She swallowed hard. Was he trying to make her melt? The spicy scent of his aftershave enveloped her. Clouded her judgment. It would be so easy to tell him how much he'd meant to her. How often she'd dreamed of a future that included the two of them navigating life's peaks and valleys together. Forever.

The front door opened.

Max cleared his throat, looking slightly flustered, then stepped back. "We should intercept them before they wake Fiona."

Hayley nodded, grateful for the distraction. They both left the kitchen, leaving behind the charged atmosphere that lingered between them. She'd almost kissed him.

As Max quietly welcomed his mom and Juliet, Hayley couldn't shake off the weight of Max's tender words. His vulnerable comment provoked her. Left her feeling both elated and anxious.

A notification pinged on her phone. She pulled it from her back pocket and checked the screen. Weston had commented on a recent selfie she'd posted.

Looking good, girl. Let's talk soon.

Her stomach tightened. Talk about *what*?

She put her phone away without responding then greeted her sister and Max's mom. "Hi there."

"Hi." Juliet's keen eyes darted between Hayley and Max. Hayley silently pleaded with her not to say a word. Juliet flashed a knowing smile before turning her attention to Fiona, who stirred in her sleep.

This wasn't the time to deal with her feelings for Max. They needed a strategy to get through the next few hours. Because Max's mother and father were about to come face-to-face, forcing Max to confront the ugliest parts of his family's past. And she had no idea how to help.

Maybe he ought to be grateful he had amnesia, because whatever had driven his parents to get divorced must have been intense. He could almost cut the tension with the knife Juliet held to serve dessert.

"Max?" Juliet paused, the sharp utensil hovering over the brownies she'd brought to the dining room table. "Would you like a brownie?"

"Yes, please."

"Cindi?" Juliet offered his mother a polite smile. "Care for a brownie or some ice cream?"

"No, thank you." Mom dabbed at the corners of her mouth with her napkin. "Hayley, the meal was delicious. I think it would be best if I leave."

"Oh, relax." Dad brought a carafe of coffee in from the kitchen. "I've made decaf. The girls brought dessert. Fiona's not crying. Why not savor a nice evening with our long-lost son?"

His mother glared daggers at her ex-husband. "In the home you've built for your new wife and daughter? I think I'll pass, Jack."

She pushed back her chair and stood. "I'm not interested in being a part of your charade." She shot one last venomous look at Dad before turning on her heel and storming toward the front door.

Max sat in stunned silence and stared after his mother. Wow. Had that really just happened? He glanced at Juliet who avoided eye contact and calmly added a scoop of vanilla ice cream to her brownie. His gaze drifted to Hayley. The concern reflected in her beautiful eyes loosened the tightness in his chest. Maybe she'd know what to say or do next?

His dad let out a heavy sigh and ran his hand through his hair. "I'm sorry about that, Max. Your mother, well, she's been through a lot."

"I'm going to walk her out." Max's chair scraped the floor as he pushed it back. "Mom, wait up."

He desperately needed to understand these fractured pieces of his past that had resurfaced. So many questions spun through his head. Had Rachel come between them? Was his mother upset about Fiona? A combination of both? His fragmented memories just kept slipping through his fingers whenever he tried to hold on to them. But he wasn't going to wait helplessly and not react while his mother fled. Clearly upset.

Max shoved his feet into his boots, plucked a coat from a hook on the wall, then hustled out the front door. "Mom, please. Don't go yet."

She'd made it down the steps and partway to

the vehicle she'd borrowed from Hayley and Juliet's brother, Wyatt. More snow had fallen in the last two hours, blanketing the SUV.

Mom turned around, her hands tucked in the pockets of her winter jacket. The silver-blue light from the bulbs mounted on the corner of the house emphasized the hurt and anger etched on her face. His stomach clenched. He could feel her pain all the way to his bones.

"Mom, what's going on? Why are you upset?"

"I'm sorry, Max." She looked away. "I tried. Really, I did. I thought I could come here tonight, and everything would be fine. And at first, it was. The meal was delicious, and Hayley and Juliet worked hard to make me feel comfortable. I'm so thankful that I get to see you again and to know that you're healthy. But I can't sit in a gorgeous house that your father built for that woman and see the baby that he had with her and pretend that my heart isn't broken over the countless ways he destroyed our family."

Her voice broke.

Oh man. "Hey, hey. Listen." His breath puffed into the cold night air. He stepped closer and pulled her into a gentle hug. "It's okay. I get it."

"I know you don't remember any of it, and this is probably all too much for you to process." She pulled back and swiped at her tears with her fingertips. "I'm sorry. It's not fair to unload on you, but I can't stay in there another minute and—"

"Stop apologizing." He cupped her shoulders with his hands. "You don't have anything to be sorry for. This is not your fault."

"I don't know what to do other than leave," she whispered.

"Please don't go back to Montana yet. I thought you planned to stay for a week? Can we get together tomorrow?"

"Not here."

"I wouldn't ask you to do that. How about if we meet for coffee or something in the morning? I have physical therapy with Hayley at her clinic at 8:30, then I'm meeting with the project manager to see what's next on the expansion."

"You have a job already?"

"It's a trade. I'm going to work on expanding the clinic in exchange for Hayley treating my ankle injury."

Mom's expression brightened. "Well, that's an unexpected but perfect arrangement."

"Why?"

"Because you and… Never mind." She gave him a tight squeeze. "I love you, Max. I'm so glad you're home."

Home. Yeah. Maybe this wasn't exactly where he belonged though.

"I love you too, Mom. Good night."

Max waited as she drove off into the snowy night. The weight of her words lingered. He hadn't asked how long Rachel and his father had been together. At least two years, based on what little information he'd gleaned from Hayley. Not that he had any right to judge, but it hurt him knowing that his mom was still so upset. And what was he supposed to do with that information?

Snow crunched under his boots as he made his way back to the house. He paused at the door, then took a deep breath before he stepped inside. The warm glow from the fireplace and lingering aromas from dinner beckoned him. Hayley sat on the couch feeding Fiona her bottle. Juliet flitted between the dining room and the kitchen, clearing the remnants of the meal.

His father was nowhere to be found.

"Everything okay?" Hayley asked softly.

Max kept his hands jammed in his jacket pockets. "I don't know. That was…a lot."

Hayley winced. "I hate that she left like that."

"Me too." He hesitated, opened his mouth and closed it again. There was a lot he wanted to say, so many questions he wanted to ask. Not to mention they'd had a moment in the kitchen earlier when they'd been alone that he wanted to revisit.

Not now, though. He rubbed his forehead with his fingertips, trying to massage away the painful ache. "Thanks for dinner. I'll see you tomorrow."

"Do you need a ride to the clinic?"

He nodded. "Please."

"Max?"

"Yeah?"

"Are you going to be all right?"

"I'll be fine. My mom's pretty upset, though, and that's hard to witness. I don't know what happened exactly between my parents. I mean, it seems like it had something to do with Rachel. Even though I can't recall the details, it hurts me that she's still so wounded."

Hayley set down Fiona's bottle, then carefully shifted the baby to her shoulder. "Your parents' divorce was tough for everyone involved."

As much as he wanted to unpack that statement, the pain in his head ratcheted up a notch, a sure sign that he needed to rest.

"Good night, Hayley." He left the house and took the path across the yard. His mother's words echoed in his head. What had happened to his family? And how could he help his mom move on?

Chapter Seven

The next afternoon, Hayley quietly entered the Butlers' house. It was only four o'clock, and if Fiona happened to be napping, she didn't want to wake her. Flames crackled in the fireplace, and a candle burning on the coffee table in the living room made the place smell like vanilla. Someone had vacuumed the carpet. Huh. The place looked great. Who'd had time to take care of a baby and do chores?

"Hey. You're off work early." Max walked into the living room, carrying a laundry basket full of clean towels. "What's going on?"

"My last two patients canceled, so I came over because we have that video call with the Spring Fling committee." She hung up her jacket. "What are you doing?"

"Helping." His dark brows scrunched together, then he set the basket on the floor and picked up the first towel from the top of the heap.

"You don't have to do that."

"Why not? I live here." He snapped the towel

in the air, sending a pleasant aroma of laundry detergent and fabric softener wafting toward her.

"I know, but I can get to it."

"But you don't have to do those chores, because I'm here. I know how to fold towels, vacuum and change diapers. It might not be exactly like you want me to, but this load will get folded."

"Where's Juliet?"

"At the store. And Fiona's napping upstairs in her crib." Max placed the folded towel on the back of the sofa.

"Wow. That's great." She pulled her laptop from her bag and set it on the coffee table. She didn't want to pick apart his contributions. His willingness to help was kind and generous. He'd already fixed the leaky faucet in the hall bathroom and patched a tiny hole in the drywall near the primary bedroom upstairs. Neither of those were tasks she or Juliet could handle, and they hadn't wanted to mention a need for repairs to Jack either. He had enough on his mind, especially after last night's blowout with Max's mother.

Hayley claimed the recliner to put some space between her and Max. While she started up her computer, she snuck a glance at him. Did he want to talk about what had happened between his parents? It wasn't really her place to explain the backstory. Max had relied on her to fill in a lot of gaps though. But if she was going to tell him the truth, she'd need to tell him everything. And she definitely wasn't ready for that.

Max turned and caught her staring. "What time is the meeting?"

She looked away and opened her email to find the link. "Four thirty. The committee chairperson is at a convention in Las Vegas, so she asked if we could meet online."

"Works for me."

A new message from Jill sat waiting in her inbox. Hayley clicked on it and scanned its contents.

"Oh no." Her chest felt tight as she read the words again. Maybe she'd misunderstood.

"What's wrong?"

"Jill just sent me a message. She heard from one of her customers at the Sluice Box that someone's made an offer on that property I want."

Max paused, a white towel partially folded in his hands. "Where you want to build the recreational venue?"

She nodded.

"What are you going to do?"

"I'll have to look for a new piece of land and pray that a generous donor comes along." She blew out a long breath. "There's nothing I can do, really. The seller's not obligated to wait for me, and I sure don't have the funds to compete with another offer."

"How much does he want?"

"He's asking $200,000, but he said he'd negotiate. He wants the land used for something that will benefit the town. Not that he has any say in the matter, the town council holds the power there regarding zoning. But I genuinely believe he wants to sell to someone with a worthy cause. Maybe the current buyer has better plans."

"Or an enticing offer." Max added the folded towel to the stack on the couch. "Have you thought about asking my dad to buy the land?"

A scoff escaped her lips before she could stop it. "No, I haven't."

"It's just an idea." He shrugged and went back to folding a towel.

Okay, so laughing at his thought had been a bit harsh. He'd already said he wanted to help, even if this latest suggestion seemed a bit far-fetched. She softened her tone. "I appreciate it. Why do you think your dad would buy land?"

"He seems like someone who is motivated by making a good impression and investing in projects that have potential." Max hesitated. "Dad and I haven't discussed it, but I had coffee with my mom today, and according to her, he inherited some money from his father. He and my mom argued about it when they got divorced, because my mom wanted to know for sure that the money would benefit me. But since he's married to Rachel, and they have Fiona, I feel Rachel's opinion counts too."

Oh boy. She really didn't want to rely on Jack Butler to solve her problems. It would be easier to figure this all out on her own. Besides, their meeting started in less than twenty minutes, and this was not the time to tell him that they'd shared this dream together. Before he'd flipped out about his father's affair and left for Peru to cope with his feelings.

"Asking your dad sounds complicated."

"Well, I guess it comes down to how serious you are about your dream."

"What's that supposed to mean?"

"I'm just saying that you seem very committed to pursuing this indoor recreational facility for the people of Opportunity, especially the kids, and I think that's amazing. If the land is up for grabs but you don't have the resources to move quickly on it, maybe it's time to ask somebody who does. My dad has a vested interest in this town."

"That doesn't mean he'll say yes."

"How do you know unless you ask?"

"It's super awkward, though. You've just given me insider information that I'm probably not supposed to know about."

"If my mom knew about it, I'm sure other people do too, so... Juicy secrets travel, right? Can't keep much under wraps around here. Or so I've been told," Max said.

"I'll think about it."

Hayley didn't know what else to say. She

couldn't stand the thought of letting her dream just die. She'd shoved it to the back burner once already. But she wasn't wealthy. She didn't have a cool million lying around. And so far, people said they were on board but had been slow to contribute. Maybe Max had a point.

Partnering with Jack Butler didn't feel right, though. Still, Anchorage had opened their facility specifically for baseball players, and it had cost them a million dollars. This project probably wasn't going to get any cheaper. She couldn't afford to wait.

Had he overstepped, suggesting that his father get involved and buy the land?

The look on Hayley's face and her instant dismissal of the suggestion rankled him. Max picked up the laundry basket full of clean, folded towels and headed for the stairs. He needed a minute to gather his thoughts. Hayley was running herself ragged, trying to meet everyone's needs. He really hated that the news about the lot had bummed her out. It bummed him out too.

Even though he had no memories of his childhood in Opportunity, he sensed that this was a great town. Sure, his mom had moved away, probably because of her contentious divorce and broken relationship with his father. Or maybe because he'd been missing for two years and she'd needed a fresh start to process her grief. He couldn't blame her for building a new life in Montana.

She had told him about many good memories from when she'd lived in Opportunity, and she still had friends here. Clearly his hometown was filled with people who looked out for one another. Evidently they liked to get in each other's business. But wasn't that true for most close-knit communities? As far as he could tell, they wanted what was best for the kids.

Max climbed the stairs slowly, grimacing at the lingering pain in his ankle, then stopped outside the linen closet in the hallway. He opened the door and neatly stacked the towels inside. On his way back toward the stairs, he paused outside Fiona's door. She'd taken a couple of naps in her crib instead of the baby swing downstairs. Hopefully that was progress, right? He just hoped she wasn't going to wake up in the middle of their meeting, at least not before Juliet returned.

He carried the empty basket to the laundry room and then went and found Hayley, who was still on the couch, frowning at her laptop.

"Anything else I can do to help?"

"No, I'm good. Just waiting for Juliet to get here so we can log on to this meeting without worrying about Fiona." She gave him a brief smile and then went right back to scrolling.

He sighed and cupped his hand on his neck.

There was so much he wanted to say, but what good would it do? "I'll be back in a few minutes."

He put on his jacket and boots and slipped out the back door. The cold evening air hit his face. He still wasn't used to these frigid temperatures after spending two years in Peru. His thoughts churned as he hurried through the snow-covered backyard. What if he reached out to his dad and asked about making a competing offer on the land? Going against Hayley's wishes left him feeling uneasy. But he couldn't *not* help. It was for the kids, after all. Maybe getting involved now meant Fiona would have a healthier, more active childhood. Surely Dad and Rachel would want to support that. So, yeah, their initial reunion had been tense, and he hadn't met his stepmother yet. He still felt a little unsure of where they stood. But now, faced with the possibility of losing what might be an important piece of Opportunity's future, he had to take action.

As he stepped inside the guesthouse, more conflicting emotions spun through him. He genuinely admired Hayley's commitment to making her hometown a better place. She deserved a chance at having her dream come true, especially one that benefited others. Max reached for the phone on the counter, then hesitated. It was a risky move, calling his father. The tension between them had been almost palpable when his mom got angry and left the dinner table during their one and only attempt at sharing a meal together. Too many unanswered questions and unspoken truths simmered. But for Hayley and for the community he was starting to care about, he'd push aside his own reservations.

He picked up the phone, thumbed through the caller ID until he found the number, then tapped the call button. A knot formed in his stomach as the phone rang. Maybe this was a terrible idea.

"Hello?"

"Dad, I need to talk to you about something important."

"I've got about seven minutes, Max. What's up?"

"Got it. Listen, there's a plot of land for sale in Opportunity. It's beside the—"

"Mr. Halverson's lot? The one diagonal from the hotel?"

Max hesitated. "I can't name the owners but yes, I'm pretty sure it's across the street from the Fairview. I found some sketches Hayley drew, and she has an incredible vision to build an indoor recreation venue for everyone to use, but especially for kids. The thing is, someone's just made an offer on that land. I'm wondering if you'd like to make a competing offer to keep it from being sold to someone who maybe doesn't have the kids' best interests at heart."

His words tumbled out in a rush. There was a long pause.

"Interesting suggestion. I'll look into it. Thanks

for calling, son. We can discuss this more when I get home tomorrow." Dad ended the call abruptly.

Max hung up, then stared at the handset. "Not the worst response ever."

Had he made a mistake reaching out? Did his proposal somehow stir up old wounds he knew nothing about? Despite the doubts creeping in, he clung to a sense of relief. At least he'd tried. Maybe this could be the first step toward healing rifts. And making a play for something precious to Hayley. Despite his sudden reappearance and memory loss, she'd been empathetic and patient. Still kept him at arm's length, though. The more time he spent with her, the more he sensed that he belonged. Here. With her. Still, he couldn't shake the nagging feeling that he might've been a little too impulsive.

"You did what?" Hayley stared at Jack. Her chest tightened. He couldn't be serious, could he?

She glanced at Max. Surely he'd intervene and tell her this was a mistake. But he leaned against the kitchen counter, holding the back of his neck. Then he met her gaze. His expression was almost imploring, as though she should be happy with this.

Juliet sat on the hardwood floor nearby, supervising Fiona's tummy time on the pastel-colored padded mat. Grunting, Fiona tried to keep her head up. Poor thing. This exercise was not her favorite.

"I bought that lot like Max asked me to." Jack pulled out a chair from the kitchen table and sat down, then leaned over and unlaced his black shoes.

"He *asked* you to?" Hayley flicked her gaze back to Max. His expression morphed into one of panic. "Max, you asked your dad to drop $200,000 on a piece of land?"

"Not quite two hundred thousand," Jack said, loosening his dark blue tie. "The Halverson family was willing to negotiate. Not only did I avoid paying the list price but I was able to secure a loan without too many hiccups. Hayley, I'd like to hear more about your proposal. I mean, in the spirit of fairness I'm not ready to commit to a singular purpose for the land, but if your idea is intriguing, I'd be inclined to give it priority."

He grinned as if he'd done her a huge favor.

Spots peppered her vision. She wanted to scream. This wasn't how this was supposed to go.

"Wow, that's…exciting." Juliet offered a weak smile. "Aren't you pumped, Hayley?"

She couldn't form a coherent sentence. Hayley pressed her palms to her cheeks. What was even happening right now? Adrenaline hummed through her veins.

"I thought this is what you wanted," Max said quietly.

"It is. I do. Um, I just—"

"You didn't expect me to get involved." Jack

chuckled as he draped his tie over the back of another chair. "That's fair. I have a reputation around here for being a bit of a villain."

"Is that why you did this?" The question tumbled out of her mouth before she could stop it, though she wasn't completely out of line in asking. Jack Butler had never done anything selfless or generous in his life. Why shouldn't she question his motives?

Jack hesitated. "To be honest, Max made a compelling argument when he said I would be investing in Opportunity's future. Which I'm all for. And being active has meant a lot to him over the years. Rachel and I want Fiona to grow up in a place where she has access to a variety of activities that your generation didn't. Selfishly I don't want Rachel to have to drive her to Anchorage or Fairbanks or send her away to expensive camps if she decides she wants to participate in sports." He held up both palms. "Getting ahead of myself, I know, since she's not even crawling yet. But when Max told me there was an offer on that piece of property and he already had sketches drawn up—"

"What sketches?" She shot Max another murderous look.

Max's brows scrunched together. "I told you, remember? I found that stuff in a box in the guesthouse. Except I didn't draw them. You did."

She tossed her hands in the air. "That was a

wild idea I sketched on the back of a napkin late at night."

"But you also said you didn't want to give up on your dream," Max said.

He was right. She didn't. Thanks to his encouragement, her dream had been revived, and Max knew it. But he still had no memory of the conversations that preceded that drawing, or the painful reality he left behind when he fled from his family's issues and chose that stupid mountain in Peru over a relationship with her. She couldn't tell him. Not here. Not in front of Juliet and his father.

Maybe not ever.

Since he'd roped his father into making her dreams come true—the man whose poor choices had been the driving force behind Max leaving town to begin with—she was feeling a little boxed in.

"I... I don't know what to say." She forced herself to look Jack in the eye. "Thank you for keeping my facility in mind for your new land."

She barely choked out the words.

"You're welcome." Jack stood. "If you ladies have things under control here, I'm going to go work out in the basement. I'll be back in about an hour."

"Have a good workout," Juliet said.

Jack left the kitchen. Max, Hayley and Juliet didn't say a word.

Less than a minute later, Jack popped back into

the room. "I'm flying to California in the morning. If all goes well, Rachel will be discharged and home in about a month or so. Just in time for the Spring Fling."

"Great." Hayley forced a smile. "Thank you for letting us know."

"No problem." Jack grinned then headed for the basement stairs.

Fiona started to fuss, and Juliet scooped her into her arms. "Your dad is full of big news today, sweetheart. Yes, he is," Juliet cooed, gently booping Fiona on the nose.

The baby cried louder.

"Alrighty then." Juliet grimaced then settled Fiona on her shoulder and patted her back.

"Yeah, that was quite the plot twist," Hayley said weakly, avoiding Max's gaze as she crossed to the fridge and retrieved a can of sparkling water. She didn't want this project to fail before it even got off the ground, but she couldn't say she was eager to partner with the Butler men, either. The sinking feeling in her stomach warned her this wouldn't end well.

Conversation flowed and silverware clinked around them as Max sat with his mother at a corner booth inside the Sluice Box. Four guys facing a television mounted on the far wall cheered for a touchdown. Max squinted to see who was playing, something that felt like it might have been a habit once. He didn't really care to keep up with the game, though. Between thoughts of Hayley and trying to stay present to enjoy his mother's last evening in town, his attention was occupied.

Jill set a triple-decker slice of ice cream pie on the table between Max and his mother. The peanut butter chocolate and vanilla layers were divided by a thin layer of fudge. A crushed chocolate cookie crust formed the foundation, and a generous swirl of whipped cream with a maraschino cherry topped it all off. Jill had drizzled chocolate syrup along the edges of the white square plate.

"Here you go, you two." She set two spoons on the varnished wood table, then placed a hand on Max's shoulder. "Danny and I are just so happy to see you sitting at one of our tables again. I can't even tell you. And Cindi, it's been great having you back in Opportunity. I'm glad you were able to make the trip."

"Aw, thank you so much, Jill." Mom tipped her head to one side. The candlelight from inside the lantern on their table made her blue eyes gleam. "Dinner and dessert with my son is the perfect finale for my visit."

Max fiddled with his coffee mug. "I'm grateful for everything my friends and family have done to welcome me back."

"I'm sure it hasn't been an easy transition but praise God that the two of you have been brought back together."

Max smiled and reached for his spoon. "God has been gracious to us all."

"Oh, and thank you again for being willing to serve on the Spring Fling royal court. The festival is a real morale booster for everybody in the community after a long hard winter. The activities help the small businesses in the area, including this one."

"Happy to do it."

More than happy, actually, because any commitment with the Spring Fling court meant more time spent with Hayley.

A server came along and hovered at Jill's elbow. "Would you like regular or decaf?"

Max and Cindi both asked for decaf.

"I'd better get back to work," Jill said. "Enjoy the Mother lode."

"The what?"

Mom's brows furrowed. "Our dessert. You don't remember it, do you." It wasn't a question.

He stifled a sigh. If he had a dollar for every time he'd heard that lately, he'd have a solid head start on his new climbing gear fund.

She didn't give him a chance to reply. "This used to be your absolute favorite."

He chuckled, stirring some cream into his coffee. "I don't know that I'm a huge fan of triple-decker ice cream pie when it's twenty-five below outside, but I'll give it a try."

"You don't drink your coffee black anymore?"

"I guess not," he said. "Hayley and Juliet have these fancy creamers in the fridge at the house. They're tough to resist."

"How are things with you and Hayley?"

Sighing, he carved off a small bite of the ice cream pie. "I think I messed up, Mom."

She tapped a packet of sugar into her coffee. "I doubt that. What's on your mind?"

"So please don't be mad, but a few days ago, I asked Dad to get involved in buying property for this venue that Hayley wants to build."

"I remember that venue. She talked about that off and on for years."

"She did?"

Mom paused, her spoon loaded with whipped cream halfway to her mouth. "Yes, honey. You were a part of those conversations as well. But did you really have to bring your father into it?"

He mentally scoured his brain for any details that aligned with what his mother said. Still nothing. Huh. "The land she wanted came on the market, and somebody made an offer. She was upset, so I thought Dad could make a competing offer, but the thing is, she's not real happy about him getting involved."

Mom pinned him with a long look.

"I know, I know." He held up his palms. "I may not remember it myself, but I get the impression that when he gets involved, things get messy. And I admit it was an impulsive move on my part."

"Is that what Hayley said?"

"Not exactly. She did question his motives, though, which I can't blame her for. It's just that… I don't have any memories of my life before, and it feels like it's blocking any relationship I might build with her now." He glanced around the restaurant with its vintage gold mining pans, framed black-and-white photos of the gold rush, and old jerseys from the high school basketball team. Even in the cozy lighting, he understood how much history mattered to his hometown. Too bad he still couldn't dig up his own.

"At the risk of sounding petty, your father's motives are often questionable. To me, the larger issue is whether Hayley wants you and your dad involved in this going forward."

"That's why I'm afraid I've made a colossal mistake. I really like her, Mom. I can tell it bothers her that I went for this and didn't pay more attention to how it affected her."

Something that looked like pain flashed across his mom's face. His gut tightened. "What is it? What did I say?"

"You and Hayley need to have a conversation, honey. I can't navigate this for you. She cared deeply for you once, and I believe that you felt the same. I know you're scared, but she's probably equally as frightened and I think it's normal for all of us that care about you to grapple with these big feelings. We thought you were gone forever and now you're back, and we're just trying to figure out how to fold you back into our lives and help you heal. I want you to be happy and if that includes Hayley, that's great. But if it doesn't, then you'll find your way through that too."

He took another bite of the massive dessert, mostly to appease his mother's nostalgia. It was tasty, but a little too sweet for his liking. Besides, he'd kind of lost interest in dessert after what she'd just said. Because the thought of a future without Hayley did not suit him at all.

Chapter Eight

"We have food left over." Annabelle gestured to the tray of sandwiches on the break room counter. "I ordered too much from the Sluice Box. Do you want to take some home?"

"Sure." Hayley smiled. "Juliet and I will eat them for dinner."

"Why don't you take some out to Max?" Garrett crumpled up his paper wrapper and tossed it in the trash can by the door.

"Oh, great idea." Annabelle's expression brightened. "Wonder what he likes."

"Turkey and provolone. No mustard," Hayley said. "Here. I'll take it to him."

"Thanks, but I'm headed that way anyway," Annabelle said.

"I've got it." Before Annabelle could argue, Hayley scooped up the sandwich.

"Don't forget chips, cookies and a drink. Whatever he wants. He's doing a great job out there," Garrett said, as he popped the top on a can of sparkling water. "Annabelle, let's go over cancellations for this afternoon and see if we can get those appointments filled."

Hayley bit back a smile. She'd hug him if he weren't her boss. She'd seen the way Annabelle had eyed Max this morning when he'd worked on his strengthening exercises, and an old, familiar jealousy swam in her gut. No, she wasn't jealous. More like protective. Max did not need an Annabelle in his life right now. Honestly, she couldn't fathom the idea of him dating anyone.

Except you.

She sucked in her breath. That wasn't going to happen either.

Nick, the other PT aide, glanced up. "Are you okay there, Hayley?"

"Yeah, why?"

"You're talking to yourself."

"I've got a lot on my mind." She passed through the gym area and headed for the door that blocked off the renovation and remodeling area from the clinic. Somehow, Garrett had managed to schedule the building's extension without knocking down the wall. He planned to add extra space for a massage therapist and wanted to include a locker room-style changing space.

Hayley moved through the door and stepped into the construction zone. "Hello?"

Max glanced up from where he was studying something on an iPad. "Hey." The easy smile he offered made warmth blossom in her chest.

"We had some lunch left over from an event we had catered over at the hospital. It's for marketing, trying to get the physicians to refer patients here. Anyway, Garrett thought you might like something."

His gaze slid to the food she held in her hands. "Sure. Thanks. I was getting hungry. Did you eat?"

"Yes. I brought this all for you." She handed him the sandwich and placed the rest of his lunch on the table.

"Wow, this is awesome." His fingers brushed against hers, and he held on to the sandwich just a little longer than necessary. Something delightful zipped up her arm. She forced herself to look away.

"You've been busy." She scanned the area. "Things are moving right along in here."

"Yeah, the rest of the crew is out grabbing lunch, but I wanted to double-check these measurements and plumbing for the changing area. It has to go in soon, but something about it just isn't right."

"I'm sure you'll figure it out."

"You want to sit with me for a few minutes? It's boring eating by myself."

She checked the time on her phone. "I can stay for a bit. My next patient isn't coming for another fifteen minutes."

"Do you like working here?"

"Uh-huh. I like being in Opportunity, period. Living and working close to my family matters a lot."

He unwrapped the sandwich and took a bite, nodding as he chewed.

"What about you?" she asked. "Do you like it here?"

"I like you." His eyes sparkled.

He was such a shameless flirt. "Well, I can't be the only thing keeping you here."

"Why not? You're not the only thing, but you're a good reason to stick around."

"Max, stop."

His expression grew serious. "What did I say?"

"You're just... You're being... Silly."

"What's silly about telling you that I like you?"

"Because..."

He reached for his drink, then asked, "Are you seeing someone?"

"No," she said, flustered.

"You have a secret engagement I don't know about?"

"There are a lot of things you don't know about, but a secret engagement isn't one of them."

"Making fun of the guy with amnesia, are we? Nice."

"No," she couldn't help but laugh. "Just saying we've been here before is all."

"Really?" His eyes dipped to her lips. He wouldn't kiss her here. Would he? They were alone for the moment, but she was at work. And Garrett had granted him a generous deal, trading physical therapy for his labor. There was no way Max would jeopardize this. Besides, she might be relieved that he was back in Opportunity and rebuilding his life, but that didn't mean she was willing to let him into her heart again.

His strong forearms flexed a little as he opened the bag of chips. "Want some?"

"No, thanks."

"What are you afraid of, Hayley?"

His question about flattened her. "What?"

"You act like someone who is afraid. Guarded. You won't let me in. Who hurt you?"

You.

She tamped down the word and hopped to her feet. "I'm going to go see if my patient's here. Sometimes they come in early. Enjoy your lunch. I'll see you back at the house. Bye."

She rushed out of there before he could say another word. That had been so close. What if he had kissed her? What would she have done? She couldn't let it happen—he'd only break her heart. She had learned that the hard way. Max was fun and flirty and made her feel like the only woman in the world. But that would only last until a big, staggering mountain caught his eye, and then he'd be gone. And there was no way she could endure losing him again.

***

He'd pushed her too far.

Max sat on the makeshift bench in the renovation area and stared at the heavy plastic sheeting draped over the opening that Hayley had just darted through. Now he'd been left alone to rehash their interaction. It wasn't the first time he'd flirted with her, but this time she'd made it clear he'd crossed the line. Some sort of boundary he didn't even recognize. Max winced. That wasn't good. And she'd called him silly. Yet he had also caught her staring at him. And she seemed to appreciate him being around, even if she did act exasperated sometimes.

So if he got under her skin so much, then why did she bring him lunch? He'd sort of hoped that she did it because she cared. But now he wasn't sure. Anyone who worked here could've delivered the food. He glanced down at the half-finished sandwich in his lap.

He did like Hayley. There was so much about her that he found attractive. She was funny and beautiful and feisty and obviously took great care of the people who mattered to her. Even though his lack of concrete memories made him question his own judgment, he wasn't wrong about one very important thing—she kept him at arm's length, and he couldn't figure out why.

A sliver of a memory flashed through his mind. He sat perfectly still, determined to capture it.

Hayley in a restaurant—the Sluice Box—standing beside him. With a pen hovering over a notepad. Was she taking his order? She'd been smiling, that part he knew for sure. More details crystalized. He'd been teasing her about... He squeezed his eyes shut.

The memory vanished.

He tightened his fist around his napkin. *No. Wait. Please.* Oh, he desperately wanted to remember more about this moment. About his life before with Hayley. He opened his eyes and looked around. An unsettling feeling lingered in the air. Part of him wanted to get up and go into the clinic and talk to her about it. To make things right. To tell her that he'd recalled something important. Finally. That one of his only memories of his life before the accident had resurfaced, and it included her. That had to mean something, right?

Except he didn't want to make her uncomfortable or interfere with her work. She'd said she had a patient coming after all. Still, this was all so frustrating. He wanted to figure out what she was afraid of, who had hurt her. To mend whatever crack had formed between them. It really bothered him to think that somebody might have broken her heart.

He crumpled his empty wrappers and tossed them in the nearby trash can, then set his drink aside. He reached for his tools, but his thoughts circled back to Hayley. Sighing, he ran a hand through his hair. Hayley was a puzzle he couldn't quite solve. Crossing the unfinished room, he pushed aside the plastic sheeting and headed into the clinic. As he entered the gym area where the patients exercised, he spotted Hayley standing near the rack of therapeutic exercise bands, typing away on her laptop. She looked up as he approached, her expression guarded.

He cleared his throat, trying to find the right words. "I feel like things got awkward just now. Can we talk?"

"For a few minutes. My patient's actually running late today." Hayley gestured toward a door leading to a quieter space. "Let's go in here."

Max followed her, the tension between them palpable. Annabelle tracked their movements from her seat behind the front desk. Yeah, they were definitely giving the rest of the staff something to talk about.

They stepped inside a small storage room with floor-to-ceiling shelves packed with shrink-wrapped bundles of white towels, boxes of athletic tape and reams of white paper. Max gently closed the door then faced her. "I wanted to apologize."

Hayley crossed her arms, her eyes fixed on Max. "For what exactly?"

Her defensive gesture didn't stop him from continuing. "I know I pushed some boundaries a minute ago, and I'm really sorry."

A mix of emotions flitted across her features.

Surprise, wariness and a hint of something else he couldn't quite decipher.

"I appreciate that." She uncrossed her arms. "You're a great guy and all, but I felt like you were prying and I need you to understand that I have boundaries for a reason."

He nodded and held her gaze. "I get it. Again, I'm sorry. It was never my intention to make you uncomfortable. It's just...a few key details have finally popped up in my mind and I think... I think you were part of my life back then. I'm just trying to piece things together."

She didn't answer. Instead, she turned and started straightening the already neatly stacked boxes of tape.

"Hayley, come on," he said, trying to keep impatience from his voice. "Don't do this. Don't turn away."

She stiffened. The air in the small room felt thick.

Slowly, she turned and faced him again. "You're right. You were part of my life before the accident," she said quietly. "We were close. Really close."

His heart hammered.

"But something terrible happened, and I've been trying to protect you...and myself." Her voice wavered and she stared at the floor.

Adrenaline spiked in his veins. He wanted to reach out and lift her chin so she would look at him. But he jammed his hands in his pockets and gave her the space she seemed to crave. "Hayley, whatever it was, we can face it together. I want to remember. I need to understand what happened between us."

"Here's the thing." She met his gaze again. "I know you're trying to remember. That's not something you can force, and no one is blaming you for your accident. But the past is complicated." She hesitated. "I'm worried that dragging it all out into the light will hurt both of us."

The layers of unspoken pain flashing in her eyes made his heart ache. "You don't have to tell me anything you're not ready to share," he said gently. "I'm here for you. Whatever you need."

Her eyes shimmered with unshed tears. "My patient is probably here by now. I don't want to keep her waiting. I have to go."

"Wait." He held his hand up. "Will you at least commit to telling me what happened before I leave on my next climb?"

Anger flashed in her eyes. Without responding, she brushed past him, opened the door and slipped out.

Max stared after her. Why was she upset? The fragments of truth she'd shared swirled in his head. So she had been a significant part of his life, and whatever had happened had left scars on both their hearts. He meant what he'd said—he wouldn't force her to share more than she was ready to. But he also couldn't ignore the connection that was still obviously pulling them together. His desire to uncover the whole truth clashed with his promise to respect her boundaries.

He took a minute to compose himself then left the storage room. The clinic buzzed with activity as patients warmed up on the treadmills and stationary bikes. Hayley was nowhere in sight.

As he headed back to work, her words pinged around in his mind.

We were close. Really close.

What did that mean? And how could they repair whatever had broken between them?

Max and Hayley stood outside the quaint general store, their table loaded with carafes of hot cocoa and coffee. The smell of freshly brewed beans mingled with the cool morning air, enticing passersby to stop and indulge. The town was buzzing with excitement as residents eagerly awaited the most popular part of the annual Spring Fling celebration—the cracking of the ice on the King River, a sure sign that spring had arrived. The sun peeked through the clouds, casting dappled light on the frost-covered ground, adding to the festive atmosphere.

But Hayley was feeling less than festive. As she poured another cup of hot cocoa, she couldn't shake off feelings of unease. Oh sure, warmer temperatures and less snow were definitely worth celebrating because the ice on the rivers breaking up meant spring wasn't far away. Summer would quickly follow, offering an end to the darkness with gorgeous sunny days. She'd eventually shed her sweaters, heavy boots, and jeans and trade them in for shorts, T-shirts and the warmth of the sun on her skin.

That all felt miles away, though, as she stood shivering at the coffee stand during the last week of March. The town was alive with excitement, chatter filling the streets as residents celebrated with games, contests, and artisans selling crafts at their booths on Main Street. Schools had been closed for the day. Children ran around with rosy cheeks and wide smiles, while adults gathered in small groups, chatting about their plans for the annual festival. Hayley stirred cream into her second cup of coffee and tried not to stare at Max. He effortlessly charmed the townspeople who came to get their hot drinks. As they chatted, she wondered if any of these faces were familiar to Max yet. Her mind kept wandering back to Max's return from the dead. Even though he'd been home for two months, it was still hard for her to wrap her head around it—one day he was gone, and now here he was standing right beside her. Would he ever recover his memories from before the accident? Sure, he'd mentioned that glimpses of his past had resurfaced in his head. A past that he now knew included her. Which had sort of freaked her out. Then he'd made it extra complicated when he'd told her he still planned to climb another dangerous mountain soon. Okay, so she wasn't proud of how she'd fled the scene—twice—at the clinic last week. Probably could've handled that whole thing better. Still. She had to protect her fragile heart. Because she wasn't ready to trust Max again.

Enough. She pushed those thoughts aside and focused on their duty for the day—serving the community and celebrating Spring Fling. The town's annual festival was a big deal, and she needed to fulfill her commitments with a cheerful attitude. Besides, she and Max still had three more events on their list of royal responsibilities: judge the kids' artwork on display at the community center, participate in the paper airplane contest and play in tomorrow's snowshoe softball game. Well, that one was just for her. Max had to sit that one out due to his ankle. He'd made a ton of progress with physical therapy, but didn't quite have the mobility to play softball while wearing snowshoes.

She smiled at longtime resident Martha Baldwin as she approached their table. "Good morning. Would you like coffee or hot cocoa?"

"Coffee, with two sugars and two creams, please." Martha rummaged in her pockets then pulled out a tissue.

"I'll leave plenty of room for cream, and let

you fix it just the way you want it." She forced a smile. "How are you, Mrs. Baldwin? Excited for spring? Any big trips planned?"

"Oh, you know, Bill and I always take the grandkids on our annual cruise."

"That sounds fun. Where are you headed?"

"Well, their spring break is just around the corner, so this year we're going to a theme park in Florida and then heading on to the Caribbean."

"Wow, you're going to have a ball. Remind me, how many grandchildren do you have now?"

"Three, with one more on the way."

"Congrats. You must be thrilled." She handed her the coffee. "Enjoy the day."

"Hayley!" a familiar voice squealed.

Hayley craned her neck to see past Mrs. Baldwin. Nicole Yates weaved through a group of people standing nearby, clutching a fancy camera.

"Nicole!" Hayley scooted past Max, skirted around the table, then flung her arms around her friend. "It's so good to see you."

Nicole pulled Hayley into a tight hug, then leaned back, grinning. "I'm so glad we ran into each other. It's been way too long."

"I know, right? How's life in Seward?"

"It's good. Really good." Nicole pointed to the hot beverage stand. "What's going on here?"

Hayley gestured to Max. "You remember Max Butler? He used to come into the restaurant all the time. We're serving hot drinks today. Can I get you something?"

"Wait." Nicole's face filled with confusion. "Max Butler? I thought—"

"It's kind of a wild story. I'll fill you in later." Hayley turned to Max. "This is Nicole Yates. She used to work as a hostess at the Sluice Box, until she got married and moved to Seward."

"Nice to see you, Nicole." Max held up an empty cup. "Coffee or cocoa?"

"Wish I could," Nicole said, holding up the camera. "But I agreed to take pictures for the town's social media account. Would you guys mind if I took a few shots of you together?"

Hayley glanced at Max. "Are you okay with that?"

He shrugged. "Why not?"

Hayley joined him behind the table again. Max draped his arm around her shoulders and pulled her close, making her pulse thrum. She felt good, tucked up against his strong, athletic frame.

"Smile, please." Nicole aimed the camera their way. "Perfect."

After Nicole lowered the camera and clicked through the images on the device, she offered another reassuring smile. "You guys look awesome. Thank you. Is it okay if I post these online later?"

"Sure," Hayley said.

"Not a problem," Max agreed. "Come back later if you decide you need a break and some cocoa."

you fix it just the way you want it." She forced a smile. "How are you, Mrs. Baldwin? Excited for spring? Any big trips planned?"

"Oh, you know, Bill and I always take the grandkids on our annual cruise."

"That sounds fun. Where are you headed?"

"Well, their spring break is just around the corner, so this year we're going to a theme park in Florida and then heading on to the Caribbean."

"Wow, you're going to have a ball. Remind me, how many grandchildren do you have now?"

"Three, with one more on the way."

"Congrats. You must be thrilled." She handed her the coffee. "Enjoy the day."

"Hayley!" a familiar voice squealed.

Hayley craned her neck to see past Mrs. Baldwin. Nicole Yates weaved through a group of people standing nearby, clutching a fancy camera.

"Nicole!" Hayley scooted past Max, skirted around the table, then flung her arms around her friend. "It's so good to see you."

Nicole pulled Hayley into a tight hug, then leaned back, grinning. "I'm so glad we ran into each other. It's been way too long."

"I know, right? How's life in Seward?"

"It's good. Really good." Nicole pointed to the hot beverage stand. "What's going on here?"

Hayley gestured to Max. "You remember Max Butler? He used to come into the restaurant all the time. We're serving hot drinks today. Can I get you something?"

"Wait." Nicole's face filled with confusion. "Max Butler? I thought—"

"It's kind of a wild story. I'll fill you in later." Hayley turned to Max. "This is Nicole Yates. She used to work as a hostess at the Sluice Box, until she got married and moved to Seward."

"Nice to see you, Nicole." Max held up an empty cup. "Coffee or cocoa?"

"Wish I could," Nicole said, holding up the camera. "But I agreed to take pictures for the town's social media account. Would you guys mind if I took a few shots of you together?"

Hayley glanced at Max. "Are you okay with that?"

He shrugged. "Why not?"

Hayley joined him behind the table again. Max draped his arm around her shoulders and pulled her close, making her pulse thrum. She felt good, tucked up against his strong, athletic frame.

"Smile, please." Nicole aimed the camera their way. "Perfect."

After Nicole lowered the camera and clicked through the images on the device, she offered another reassuring smile. "You guys look awesome. Thank you. Is it okay if I post these online later?"

"Sure," Hayley said.

"Not a problem," Max agreed. "Come back later if you decide you need a break and some cocoa."

"I will." Nicole pinned Hayley with a meaningful look. "We have to catch up. Soon."

"I'll text you." Hayley waved. "See you later."

"Wouldn't it be great if you created a social media account to tell people about your brand-new venue?" Max angled his head toward the empty lot down the street that his father had purchased last month.

Hayley avoided eye contact and focused on wiping up droplets of coffee and cocoa from the table, then checked to make sure plenty of stir sticks were available. "I'd love to tell more people about the venue. The thing is, your dad hasn't been available to talk over business plans, interview an architect, or go to a town council meeting to request a zoning change. I'm supposed to find out this week if I got the grant I applied for. At this rate, it will be two more years until we celebrate with a grand opening. So it's a little soon to create a social media account for a venue that doesn't exist."

"Here's more sugar packets." Max handed her a package to restock the small bin of sweeteners. "You think it's going to take that long to build it?"

Hayley stomped her feet on the sidewalk to warm up her frigid toes. "I'm trying to be realistic."

What else could she say? Of course she longed for the day when they could promote their new venue and share it with the world. Still, she couldn't help feeling resentful toward Max's father for swooping in and taking over her dream. Their dream. Jack was being more of a roadblock than an asset at this point, because he hadn't officially agreed to the indoor venue. Part of her worried he had plans to bring a developer in and put up something completely unrelated.

She struggled to keep her composure as she wiped up the mess on the table. Lashing out at Max wouldn't help. At all. Oh, how she longed to tell him everything—how betrayed she felt. How disappointed she was that he'd walked away from her and her dream without a second thought. Instead, she fought to keep her emotions in check because all she wanted was for Max to remember their past and understand how much his absence had hurt her.

You can't keep ignoring your feelings.

Sighing, she banished that unhelpful reminder. Yeah, okay, so pretending everything was fine wouldn't make the conflict disappear, no matter how hard she tried to convince herself otherwise. But that still didn't change the fact that Max hadn't regained his memories so he didn't remember all that he'd abandoned. He'd left town in a desperate attempt to cope with his family falling apart. Didn't that deserve a little of her empathy?

Maybe she should tell him now. Finally get all her messy, complicated feelings out in the open. Inform him plain and simple that she couldn't let herself hope for anything because he'd already proven to her that she wasn't enough for him.

Except she couldn't bring herself to say it. One small part of her still felt like that was really cruel, almost like rubbing salt in the wound.

Max tossed an empty cardboard box in the recycle bin behind them. "Are you looking forward to the dance?"

She hesitated. "Yeah, I haven't been to one in a few years." In fact, she'd avoided the Spring Fling formal since Max had disappeared.

"Really?" His eyebrows raised. "That's hard to believe."

Max's response surprised her. Hayley shrugged it off. "It's no big deal. I just haven't been asked, that's all."

"I don't know what those guys are thinking," Max joked. "They must be blind not to see how amazing you are."

A blush crept up her cheeks. She couldn't deny that it felt nice for Max to say that about her.

"Thanks," she said.

Max held her gaze. "I'm looking forward to dancing with you, Hayley. If you want to, that is."

What was he doing, flirting like this? And why was she so powerless to resist him? Her pulse sped up as she tried to push down her conflicting feelings. They only seemed to grow stronger. The air between them crackled with unspoken words and unresolved emotions. Oh, how she longed for the connection they once shared, for the easy laughter and comfortable companionship that had defined them before everything changed.

Would dancing with him rekindle old flames or simply fan the embers of a love that had never truly burned out? With a mixture of anticipation and trepidation, Hayley nodded slowly.

"I'd like that, Max. One dance."

What could it hurt? After all, as part of the royal court they'd be expected to appear as a couple. Maybe even dance together a few times. Surely she could handle that. Besides, it was three days away. Plenty of time to figure out how to reinforce her friends-only boundaries.

Chapter Nine

"Only a few more minutes, pretty girl, then both your parents will be home."

Max sat on the floor in the living room with Fiona next to him. A full bottle that she'd refused sat on the coffee table. "At least you napped."

She squirmed, arching her back, and twisting onto her side as she lifted her head from the colorful mat. Her face flushed pink. He'd spent enough time with her to know that if she didn't get what she wanted the crying would likely start soon.

"You're a tummy time rock star. You've almost got this rolling over thing figured out. How about if I give you a little help?" He gently rolled her over onto her back. Fiona kicked her legs and punched the air with her adorable fists. Then her blue eyes locked on the stuffed animals in colorful shapes suspended on the mobile over her head. She cooed, and the tense knot in his stomach loosened.

"Since Hayley and Juliet aren't here, I get to be in charge. At least for a few minutes. I'm not going to let you get all worked up five minutes before your mom walks in the door."

Besides, he was worked up enough for both of them. His father and Rachel were coming home. He kind of wished Hayley was here, but she and her sister had insisted he ought to handle this reunion on his own. This was the first time he would experience getting together as a family of four. Him, his dad, his stepmother and his baby sister. Plus, he didn't want to do anything to upset Rachel. She was apparently doing well and had been discharged a week earlier than expected, but it had to be daunting traveling from California to Alaska, knowing she'd need to ease back into motherhood. He wasn't a woman or a mother, but he could certainly relate to the challenges of moving home and reentering normal life. What if she had a relapse? What if her postpartum depression hadn't been resolved?

He stood and walked to the window, glanced down at the empty driveway, then nervously paced the floor. Fiona fussed, so he tapped the white noise machine nearby, which filled the room with calming sounds of ocean waves. She stared up at the stuffed whale dangling over her head. Thankfully, the crying stopped.

A few minutes later, the rumble of a car pulling up outside the house tugged him back to the window. Adrenaline zipped through his veins. He drew some deep, calming breaths. His father climbed out of the car, and a woman who had to be Rachel got out on the passenger side. Wow, she was young. He knew they only had an eleven-year age difference but seeing her in real life clarified the fact that he had a stepmother who wasn't old enough to be his mother.

Oh, Dad. Nope, he wasn't going to think about how Rachel might've led to his parents' failed marriage or how much his father's behavior had harmed his mother. Today was about Rachel and helping her get settled comfortably.

His father and Rachel came inside the house. Her thick honey-colored hair hung in a long braid, and she wore a mint green puffer jacket, trendy jeans and tall boots. Even with very little makeup on, she was a stunning woman.

"Hello, Max." She blinked back tears. "It's so good to see you again."

He walked toward her. "Hello, Rachel. Welcome home."

They exchanged an awkward hug. She pulled away and her gaze darted to Fiona. She sucked in her breath. "Oh, my baby girl, she's so big."

Rachel quickly took off her jacket and thrust it toward Jack. "How are things here, Max?"

His father took the jacket and hung it up without speaking.

"Things are good." Max jammed his hands in the front pocket of his hoodie. "How was your trip?"

Rachel crossed the room and sank to her knees on the floor, then scooped Fiona up and held her close, whispering softly.

"Uneventful." Dad offered a tight smile before shrugging out of his own jacket.

"Good. Glad to hear it." He rocked back on his heels. Wow, this was awkward. Did they expect him to hang around, or did they want to be alone?

Rachel gently rocked Fiona in her arms as tears slid down her pink cheeks. Uh oh. Max winced. A mix of emotions swirled inside. Relief that Rachel seemed glad to be back home, gratitude that his father had helped his wife get the help she needed and a lingering sense of guilt for the hurt he worried his absence had caused in their lives.

As Rachel cooed to Fiona, Max felt a surge of protectiveness wash over him. He wanted to shield his stepmother and half sister from any harm or pain, to be the anchor they needed in this new family dynamic. Despite the tangled web of emotions and history between them all, he was determined to make things work.

His father stood by the doorway, watching the trio with a soft smile on his face. Jack's eyes met Max's. Did they both want what was best for Rachel and Fiona, even if it meant navigating through past mistakes and heartaches? The weight of their shared history hung in the air around them. A history he couldn't quite grasp yet. And maybe he never would. But that wouldn't stop him from doing his best to make life easier for his family.

"Thank you for being here, Max," Rachel whispered, her voice barely above a breath. "I know this isn't easy for you."

"You're welcome. I'm glad to help out. Hayley and Juliet are the real heroes, though. They've been super helpful."

She gave Max a watery smile. "I'm grateful for the support you've all shown us while I've been away."

Rachel gently rocked Fiona, who had started to doze off in her arms. Jack nodded in agreement, a proud glint in his eyes as he watched Rachel interact with Fiona. "We're all in this together now."

Was that a hint of vulnerability in his voice? Max felt a surge of gratitude toward his father for the first time in a long while. Despite the rocky past and the lingering wounds, seeing Jack embrace this new chapter with sincerity gave him hope. Maybe, just maybe, they could heal as a family.

The decorating committee had gone all out. Hayley stood at the edge of the dance floor inside the community center and turned in a slow circle. A disco ball spun from the ceiling, sprinkling rainbow confetti lights across the worn squares of the parquet dance floor. Clear strands of lights framed each of the four rectangle windows, and people sat at round tables spread around the room. Flickering candles, small vases filled with red and white carnations and wrapped pieces of candy served as centerpieces. Platters of sweet and savory hors d'oeuvres and a three-tiered cake sat beside giant containers of iced tea, lemonade and coffee lined the far wall. Someone had hired a DJ from Fairbanks, and upbeat pop music thumped from the oversize speakers on either side of his station at the edge of the dance floor.

She waved to Nicole, who was making the rounds with her camera, then smoothed her hands over the A-line skirt of her sage green dress. Juliet had convinced her to get her nails done, and her hair styled in a fancy twist. Nora over at the Golden Curl Salon had done a fantastic job. Okay, so maybe it was a tiny bit fun to get dressed up. She hadn't been excited to put in the extra time, money and effort, but her sisters had reminded her that as part of the Spring Fling court, all eyes would be on her. Still, she couldn't wait to get back home, put on some leggings, a T-shirt and her favorite cozy cardigan, and watch a sweet made-for-TV movie.

Max paused beside her. She couldn't help but sneak another appreciative glance. He looked good. Really good. His bright blue suit paired with a crisp white button-down and casual leather loafers made her pulse thrum. Had he raided his father's closet? She'd never seen him wear anything like this or look so handsome.

Okay, settle down.

There had to be at least half a dozen women staring at him right now, though. Impulsively, she tucked her hand in the crook of his elbow.

He glanced down and his mouth curved in a grin. "Hey there."

"Hi."

"You look beautiful tonight."

She dipped her chin. "Thank you. You're looking quite handsome as well."

His gaze slid to her hand on his arm. "What are you doing? Staking your claim?"

Heat singed her cheeks. "More like protecting you."

"From what?"

"The onslaught of single women who are about to stampede over here and drag you onto the dance floor."

His expression grew serious. Something she couldn't quite identify flickered in his eyes.

"You're the only woman I want to dance with, Hayley."

"I did promise you a dance."

"Well, come on then." He started toward the dance floor. "I'm ready."

"We should hydrate first." Hayley tugged him toward the drink station. Maybe some lemonade would quell the nerves swarming like bees in her tummy.

Mrs. Baldwin stepped into their path. Oh, boy. Hayley stifled a groan. She should've known they wouldn't be allowed to stay alone for long.

"Max and Hayley, so glad you could join us tonight," she said. "We appreciate you serving your community on the royal court."

"We're happy to be here," Max said. "You look lovely in blue, by the way."

Mrs. Baldwin splayed her hand across her blue sequined top. "Thank you so much, Max. What a sweet fellow you are." She tucked her long straight gray hair behind her ear. "Once everyone is here and had time to eat, members of the court will proceed into the middle of the dance floor for a brief ceremony, so don't run off."

"Wouldn't dream of it," Hayley said sweetly.

After Mrs. Baldwin walked away, Max turned to face her.

"Why do I get the feeling that you'd rather be anywhere else but right here?"

Were her emotions that transparent? Instead of answering, she let her eyes wander to his jawline. He'd neatly trimmed his beard, and the lines at the corners of his eyes crinkled as he offered another impish grin.

"Am I right?"

She blew out a long breath, then steered him to the drink station and got herself a lemonade.

"To be honest, I'd rather be watching a movie or playing with Fiona."

It was true. Watching Fiona kick her adorable little feet while she stared at her mobile or sitting by the fire and building a puzzle sounded far more enjoyable than being stared at in this crowded room. Not that she wouldn't enjoy dancing with Max, letting him hold her in his strong arms. The problem was, she'd likely enjoy it too much.

Max angled his head and pinned her with a long look. Did he suspect that her attraction toward him had grown?

He reached past her to grab a napkin and a ham and cheese slider, his sleeve brushing her bare arms. Electric tingles hummed across her skin. "It's funny how much I miss her, considering I just saw her."

"I'm sure Rachel and your dad are taking good care of her. How's Rachel doing, by the way?"

Max shrugged. "So far, so good. We'll see. She has to check in with her new psychiatrist in Anchorage next week."

Hayley tossed her empty cup in the trash can at the end of the table. "I'm glad she's home."

Max finished chewing, then wiped his mouth with his napkin. "Come on. Let's dance."

"But what about Mrs. Baldwin and her official ceremony?"

Max craned his neck to survey the crowd. "She's busy chatting, so we have time for at least one dance before the will of the people is revealed and the king and queen are announced."

"I'm not sure we're going to be able to live with you and your ego if you are chosen to be the king," Hayley teased.

"I'm going to boast about it for decades."

"You're for sure a people person. I know you'll bask in all the extra attention."

His brows scrunched together. "Was I a guy who typically drew a crowd?"

She couldn't help but chuckle. "Absolutely. You held court at your table at the restaurant all the time."

"I did?"

"Oh yeah. Climbers were totally into you. They hung on every word you said."

His cheeks flushed pink. "No."

"It's true."

He held out his hand. The playful gleam had returned to his eyes. "Enough about that. Let's pretend to be royalty celebrating spring in Alaska."

Her heart fluttered and she hesitated. But as she looked into Max's eyes, she saw nothing but kindness and warmth. So she placed her hand in his and let him lead her to the center of the dance floor.

As they swayed together, peace washed over her. For a moment, all her doubts and worries faded away and she savored being in this moment with Max holding her close. She couldn't ignore the feeling of warmth spreading through her. Maybe things weren't so complicated between them after all. She felt a rush of emotions. Confusion, longing, hope. She had spent so long trying to suppress her feelings for Max, burying them deep within her heart to protect herself from getting hurt again. But now, as her eyes locked with his, she couldn't ignore the spark of something rekindling within her.

Hayley looked stunning.

Max kept one hand on the curve of her waist, his other hand clasped in hers. The warmth of her palm pressing into his as they danced made every minute of his arduous recovery worth it. A wisp of her auburn hair had slipped from the complicated twist at the back of her head. He resisted the urge to reach up and tuck it behind her ear.

They turned in slow circles on the dance floor in the community center, a popular ballad playing through the speakers nearby. When he was stuck in Peru, he'd make up scenarios in his head about what it might be like to come home. Whatever home meant. He hadn't imagined anything as enjoyable as this. A beautiful woman dancing with him, and a community of people coming together to celebrate a fresh start and a new season.

He glanced down and admired the appealing blush on her cheeks, her cute, upturned nose and the glint of light reflected in her sparkly jewelry.

Had they really only been friends? Plenty of folks around here, including his own mother, had implied they'd been more. He spotted Mrs. Baldwin weaving among the tables. She was probably headed toward the DJ's station to announce the Spring Fling king and queen. Selfishly, he didn't want this song to end because he didn't want to miss out on even a second of dancing with Hayley.

He guided them in another slow circle, smiling as he moved past Jasper and his wife, and then Savannah with Jasper's twin brother, Levi, dancing nearby.

"Everyone seems to be having a great time," he said.

"Including me." Hayley smiled at him and he nearly stumbled. "You're a good dancer."

Her compliment paired with the sweet curve of her lips made his heart kick against his ribs. How he longed to pull her close. Maybe even share a kiss. He couldn't though. Not here in front of everyone she knew. Besides, she'd given him no indication that it was what she wanted. Well, other than tucking her hand in his elbow when they first got to the dance. He would not do one thing to damage the comfortable relationship they'd established.

Besides, he still had three more sessions as her patient at the clinic, and if he kissed her now, things might get awkward. He really wanted to complete the treatment plan for his ankle and concentrate on the clinic's expansion. Keeping his word to Garrett meant a lot. Plus, he fully intended to climb Denali in May.

What was he supposed to do with these feelings though?

The warmth unfurling in his chest as he breathed in the floral scent of her now-familiar perfume, or the way he wanted to hold her for at least six more songs, twirl her around the dance floor and pretend that she was his. Not that he was in any shape at all emotionally to pursue a relationship. His mother had asked him to consider what he'd do if his memories never came back. She had a valid point. Sooner or later, he had to move on. Coming back to Opportunity was supposed to be a fresh start. He certainly didn't want to be single forever, and caring for Fiona had unlocked something wonderful inside him. A longing he hadn't known existed. He wanted to be a dad, despite his rocky relationship with his own father. Yeah, okay, he still had some unresolved issues to work through there.

The song ended, and Mrs. Baldwin stepped up to the microphone. "Folks, welcome to Spring Fling. We're so glad you're all here. Sorry to interrupt the fun. I promise this won't take long. Would all six couples in the royal court please make their way to the center of the dance floor. We'll crown our king and queen, based on your votes."

Mrs. Baldwin introduced all six couples, including Max and Hayley. He squeezed Hayley's hand as they scooted over and fanned out in a semicircle on the dance floor.

"Good luck, Jason and Calista," Hayley said to the couple standing closest to them. "You both look amazing tonight."

"Thanks." Jason grinned, then planted a quick kiss on Calista's cheek. "We've been looking forward to this all week."

"Drumroll please, Mr. DJ."

The DJ smiled and tapped a few buttons, then a simulated drumroll poured from the speakers.

Mrs. Baldwin smiled. "Friends, I'm pleased to announce that this year's king and queen of the Spring Fling are Max Butler and Hayley Morgan!"

The crowd cheered. Someone punctuated the noise with a robust whistle.

Hayley grinned at him. "Wow, this is quite an honor."

Two teenage girls came forward and draped a satin sash over Hayley and handed her a bouquet of pink roses. Then one of the girls pinned a sparkly tiara on top of Hayley's head, and the other girl gave him a velvet crown with faux rhinestones. He held it awkwardly in place.

"Wait, wait. Don't start dancing yet," Mrs. Baldwin said. "We need pictures."

She handed the DJ the microphone, then gathered all the couples in the court for a group photo.

When they'd finished and dispersed, Max handed off his crown to Jasper. Hayley asked one of the girls to hold her bouquet. The DJ started another romantic song, and Max gently pulled Hayley into his arms.

"I knew we'd win," he said.

Hayley laughed. "You did not."

"Okay, but I hoped."

She shot him a questioning look. "Why?"

"Because it means I get to dance with you again."

Hayley blushed at his words. Her gaze softened as she looked up at him. The warmth in her eyes sent an arrow of hope arcing through his heart. Maybe there was a chance for something more between them after all. As they swayed to the music, he couldn't help but steal more glances at her radiant features, illuminated by the soft glow of the mirrored ball overhead.

When she leaned into him and rested her cheek on his chest, he offered a silent prayer of thanks heavenward. The people around them faded away until there was only her. Every touch, every smile shared between them tonight made his affection grow deeper. It felt so right, holding her close like this. Together, they'd helped care for Fiona until his dad and stepmother came home. Hayley had been the one who had been a constant presence during his recovery, cheering him on through every small victory and setback. He admired the way she made everyone around here feel cared for.

She was more than a friend—she was someone he could see himself building a life with.

He wasn't quite sure how to put his feelings into words. At least not here. For now, he'd bask in the quiet joy of holding her close.

Loud commotion at the entrance caught his attention. Cold air swept into the warm room as the doors swung open. A man, tall and lean, with a rugged handsomeness that drew immediate attention strode across the room.

Hayley stiffened in his arms. Surprise flickered across her face. When the man spotted Hayley, he quickly approached them. Who was this guy? His protective instincts kicked in as he faced the newcomer, sizing him up with a quick glance. There was something about the stranger's confident demeanor that set Max on edge.

Hayley swallowed hard. "Wh-what are you doing here?"

"I came with some friends to see the northern lights. Then I heard about the Spring Fling so I couldn't resist coming to see the festivities for myself. Who knew you'd be the belle of the ball?"

The man seemed a little unsteady on his feet. Had he slurred his words?

"And who do we have here? Max, right? Hayley told me about you. Except I thought you were dead."

Hayley groaned.

Max's grip on Hayley tightened imperceptibly

at the way the man addressed him. There was an underlying tone in his words that made his scalp prickle. He forced a polite smile. "And you are?"

The man's chuckle grated on Max's nerves. "Where are my manners? I'm Weston. Hayley and I go way back."

Hayley's eyes darted between the two men. "Weston and I went to school together and dated for several months. Until he moved to California."

"But I couldn't stay away any longer, darling. 'Specially since you're ignoring my texts. I had to see you." Weston leered, then stumbled forward and tried to grab Hayley's arm.

"Nope." Max stepped between Weston and protectively nudged Hayley behind him.

Anger crossed Weston's face. He reeled back then slugged Max in the nose.

Max staggered as pain exploded across his face. The room spun as he fought to stay on his feet. The shock of the punch reverberated through him, but the instinct to protect Hayley was stronger.

Weston's expression twisted into a hideous smirk. "I should've never left. You belong with me, not some head case like him."

Voices buzzed around them. Apprehension rippled through the crowd.

Rage burned through Max as he wiped away the blood trickling down his lip. He squared his shoulders, ready to defend against another attack. "Hayley doesn't belong to anyone, least of all you."

Spots peppered his vision. He took a deep breath and steadied himself. There was no way he'd give this guy the satisfaction of passing out.

"Max?" Hayley's panicked voice sounded far away.

He reached back and found her hand, giving it a reassuring squeeze. Ignoring the dizziness, he locked eyes with Weston. The possessive gleam in the other man's eyes sent adrenaline coursing through Max. Without hesitation, he stepped forward, his hand still clasped in Hayley's as he shielded her from Weston's menacing presence. The room fell silent, all eyes on the confrontation unfolding at the center of the dance floor. Jasper, Wyatt and Jason all worked their way closer, quietly moving in behind Weston.

"Like I said, you have no claim over Hayley." Max kept his voice steady despite the throbbing pain in his nose. He swiped at the blood still dripping onto his face. "She's free to decide who she wants in her life."

Weston barked out a cynical laugh. "And you're delusional if you think she's gonna give you a second chance now."

What? His words landed like another stinging blow.

Hayley stepped around Max, her chin tipped up

in defiance. "I am not yours, Weston. We haven't been a couple for a long time. You need to leave."

Before Weston could make another move, Wyatt and Jasper grabbed him by the shoulders. "Let's go." Jasper's voice was low but filled with authority. Jason gestured for the onlookers to move back.

"Come on." Wyatt helped steer Weston toward the exit. "Get out of here before Max presses charges for assault."

Once Weston was gone, Max turned and pulled Hayley into his arms. "Are you all right?"

She leaned against his chest and looped her arms around his waist. The warmth of her embrace chased away the lingering unease.

Hayley stepped back and offered a weak smile. "I'm fine. Just a little shaken. Thank you for defending me."

"Of course." He tenderly brushed a strand of hair from her cheek. "I'll always stand up for you."

Her smile faded as she scanned his face. "You're still bleeding. Let's get you cleaned up."

"Wait." Max refused to move. "What was he talking about? The thing he said about no second chances?"

She hesitated. "Let's not focus on the past right now."

But he couldn't let it go. Not with the shadow of hurt lingering in her eyes. "I want to know, Hayley. Please."

Chapter Ten

Her insides churned as she struggled to find the right words to placate Max. Sidestepping his questions didn't feel right in the face of all that had happened. But having an intense conversation in the middle of all this chaos wasn't fair either. He wasn't budging, though. And that pleading look in his eyes chipped away at her defenses. Hayley glanced toward the front door where a group of people from the Spring Fling planning committee stood chatting in a circle. Jasper, Wyatt and Mrs. Baldwin huddled with two other members, their gestures animated. Had anyone called the police? Did Max need to press charges?

"Hayley?" Max's voice broke through her thoughts, pulling her back to reality. "We can't not talk about this."

She hesitated. He wasn't wrong.

"Folks, how about an upbeat pop song to kick-start the second half of this fling?"

The DJ's smooth baritone voice blaring from the speakers made her flinch. Had he already been instructed to keep the dance going? The crowd had mostly dispersed, but people were still shooting curious looks their way. A few even moved toward them as a new song began.

"Come on, let's make sure your nose isn't broken, and then we can find a quiet place to talk." She took his arm and led him off the dance floor, guiding him through the crowded room toward the kitchen at the opposite end of the community center.

Four women stood at the counter in the galley-style kitchen, replenishing platters of food and mixing more lemonade. When Hayley and Max appeared in the doorway, all conversation stopped. Mrs. Carter turned from dumping a cup of sugar into the lemonade, then wiped her hands on a dish towel. "Can I get you some club soda for that stain on your suit, and an ice pack for your face?"

"Yes, please." Max touched his fingertips to his cheek. "I can feel it starting to swell."

Hayley winced. Poor guy. The last thing he needed was another injury. Especially one that involved his head.

"Part of me wished you would have hit him back," Mrs. Callahan said.

One side of Max's mouth tipped up in a tentative smile. "I wanted to, but honestly, he caught me off guard. Besides, I was more concerned about protecting Hayley."

He turned to face her, his expression so earnest, and her heart nearly cleaved in two. Oh, this sweet man. How was he going to feel when she told him all the hurtful things he'd said to her? Or that his parents' marital issues had bled over into their relationship.

"Here." Mrs. Carter gave her a warm, damp paper towel. "I'll get that club soda."

She scooted past them then opened the fridge.

"Let me help." Hayley reached up and dabbed carefully at the dried blood on his face.

Max grimaced.

"Sorry," she said quietly. "Am I pressing too hard?"

"It's okay. I can deal with it." His eyes searched her face, and her skin warmed under his careful study. The air around them nearly crackled. Someone cleared their throat.

"Why don't we carry these platters out and make sure there's plenty of cake, ladies." Mrs. Carter handed Hayley a small bag of crushed ice, club soda and a clean white dish towel. "We'll give you two a few minutes."

Once they were alone, Hayley wiped the blood from her own arm then busied herself by dabbing the club soda on the droplets of blood spattered on his blue suit. He gently clasped his hand over her wrist. She sucked in a breath, then dragged her gaze to meet his.

"I need to know the truth. Was Weston right or just running his mouth?"

She dropped her gaze, then set the towel aside and twisted the cap onto the club soda bottle.

"Max, I've wanted to tell you the truth. All of it."

"Then why did it take Weston barging in here and slugging me for you to finally get around to telling me?"

Hayley gasped. Anger lit like a struck match. "You wanted me to just tell you everything? Right away, when you were grappling with not knowing anyone and not having any memories and dealing with all the drama of people realizing you weren't dead, I was supposed to just pile on? When you yourself asked for only small amounts of information, and every time you tried to remember something it seemed to hurt you?"

Max picked up the bag of ice and pressed it to his cheek. Weston had slugged him hard. "Why did he say you wouldn't give me a second chance?"

"Max, don't do this," she whispered. "I've tried so hard to protect you, and—"

"I didn't ask you to protect me." He dropped his hand to his side, then blew out a long breath. "Tell me the truth, Hayley."

Oh. She stepped back and leaned against the counter. "But we're supposed to protect the people we..." She trailed off. Stopped herself from dropping the L-word. She swallowed hard. "People we care about. Like you protected me from Weston."

His gaze narrowed. "Tell me."

She held up her palms. "All right. Here goes. You and I were friends…very good friends. Then your dad and Rachel…they had an affair while he and your mom were still married. And it turned out that it wasn't the first time he'd cheated. Your mom was crushed, and you both were understandably upset. But then you shut me out. We had all these plans for the indoor rec center and how we were going to make Opportunity a better place for kids. Then you packed your climbing gear and left for Peru."

Max's jaw clenched. His eyes darkened as her words sank in, and he gripped the counter's edge for support. "I—I know my words don't mean much given I can't remember saying or doing any of that, but please know that I would never intentionally hurt you."

"I'm sure that from your perspective now, you didn't mean to hurt me, Max. But you did. And it wasn't just about leaving—it was about the way you left, the way you cut me out of your life without a second thought."

Silence hung between them, heavy and suffocating.

Max's expression shifted from confusion to a mix of pain and regret. He opened his mouth to speak, but no words came out.

Taking a deep breath, he finally found his voice. "I'm sorry, Hayley."

Hot tears pressed against her eyes. "I know you are, Max. And I forgive you. But forgiveness doesn't erase the hurt or the past."

He closed his eyes briefly, as if trying to hold on to the fleeting moment of connection between them. When he opened them again, a quiet resolve shimmered in their depths.

"I want to make things right," Max said, his voice steady.

"Max, Hayley?" Mrs. Baldwin came into the kitchen. "The police are here. They need statements from both of you."

Max and Hayley exchanged weary looks.

"All right," Hayley said.

Max swept the air with his hand. "After you."

Without a word, they followed Mrs. Baldwin out of the kitchen and toward the two uniformed officers waiting in the community center entrance. Hayley's mind reeled from the emotional whirlwind that had swept through. The pain of the past and uncertainty about their future weighed heavy. She stole another glance at Max as they approached the officers waiting to take their statements. Although she'd been honest, she'd chosen her words carefully. There was still so much he didn't know. So what was she supposed to do now?

The next morning, Max sat in his father and stepmother's kitchen, staring into his second cup of coffee. A half-finished bowl of cereal and a banana peel sat on the table in front of him. He hadn't been too interested in eating, but he had to do something about the persistent headache. He'd hoped caffeine would help, along with the recommended dose of over-the-counter pain relievers for the throbbing pain in his face. Man, that Weston had really smacked him hard.

His father came into the kitchen.

"Good morning. How are you feeling?"

"Not great." Max sipped his coffee, wincing at the slightly bitter taste. He hadn't bothered with fancy creamers or sugar this time. Skipping the sweet stuff Hayley liked didn't banish her from his thoughts, though. She'd said he'd hurt her when he shut her out.

Why? Why had he been so thoughtless?

He shifted his gaze toward his father, standing at the counter and pouring himself a mug of coffee.

"Dad, I want to talk to you about something."

"Good. There's something I'd like to share as well." He pulled out a chair across from Max and sat down. Fiona's muffled cries wafted downstairs. Rachel's footsteps made the floors overhead creak.

"You first," Max said.

"Some friends of mine in Anchorage owe me a favor. I gave them buddy passes for a round-trip flight to Hawaii last Christmas. Anyway, he's a neurologist and says he can work you in first thing Monday morning. I'm happy to drive us to town this afternoon."

Max shifted in his seat. He didn't like where this was going. "What's the reason for the appointment?"

"You need to be seen by a neurologist, son, especially after getting hit in the head again last night."

"I didn't sustain another brain injury. The guy just punched me in the face."

Dad raised his eyebrows, then sipped his coffee without saying anything.

Okay, that did sound a little silly. Maybe he should be seen by a professional. Especially since he still had a headache. "How long will it take?"

"Probably a couple of hours. They'll most likely do an examination, then maybe X-rays or a CT scan. I'm not exactly sure."

"I don't have insurance, and that sounds expensive."

"Don't worry about it. Like I said, he owes me, and I'll pay whatever I need to out of pocket. We'll all rest easier knowing you've received adequate follow-up care."

Max sighed. He didn't have the energy to come up with any more excuses. "I'll go on one condition."

Dad's gaze narrowed. "Which is?"

"I want you to tell me why you think I left for Peru."

"Pardon?"

"Last night, right before they dragged that Weston guy out, he said that I shouldn't get a second chance. Some people have told me that I hurt them when I left the way I did. So now I want to know if it's true that I left town because I was mad at you for cheating on Mom."

Dad's face turned pale. He slumped back in his chair, then he nodded. "Yes. That is why you left."

"I just walked away from everything?"

Dad hesitated. "Define everything. To my knowledge, you had no expeditions booked here in Alaska, so you bought a one-way ticket to Peru, took your gear, told me you never wanted to speak to me again and off you went."

Hayley's pained expression flashed in his mind. Max shoved his fingers into his hair. "That's what I was afraid of."

"To be honest, I don't really blame you."

"You don't?"

His dad shook his head. "What I did to your mother was wrong. I'd cheated on her before, and she put up with a lot. I've apologized. I don't expect her to ever forgive me. This time, with Rachel, I'm trying to do what I can to make things right moving forward."

Huh. How ironic that he and his dad had a similar goal. Max kept that part to himself.

"I'm sorry, Max. I was wrong. I made some poor choices, and I regret that my shortcomings drove you away from your home."

"Apology accepted," Max said. "It might take me a while to work through all of this."

"Did you speak to Hayley about why you left?"

Max twisted his coffee mug in a slow circle. "A little bit. Then we got interrupted."

"She was pretty upset when you left."

"Yeah, I heard."

His dad pulled his phone from his pocket. "So I can text my friend and let him know you want to be seen on Monday?"

Max stood and pushed back his chair. "Let's do it."

He carried his bowl and mug to the sink, then tossed the banana peel in the trash can. He wasn't sure what good might come from the appointment, but he also wasn't going to turn down a thorough evaluation from a specialist. Especially if this neurologist could offer a definitive answer to Max's lingering question—would he ever regain his memories?

Hayley snagged the last empty parking spot, then walked toward the entrance to the Riverside Café on Sunday after church. Her mother had placed an order for a dozen bacon, egg, and cheese biscuits, fresh fruit and blueberry muffins for their family meal. Hayley had offered to stop and pick it up, even though part of her wanted to skip lunch and take a long afternoon nap instead. She desperately needed a day off to recharge after everything that had happened at the dance. The way her conversation with Max had ended still bothered her. But after they'd given their statements to the police and Max had decided not to press charges against Weston, they'd gone their separate ways.

She and Juliet had stayed up into the wee hours last night, rehashing every single detail. An email had landed in her inbox sometime during the dance, letting her know she'd received the grant she'd applied for. So she'd been even more amped up and unable to sleep. Then her alarm rang way too early, and she'd dragged herself out of bed because she'd previously agreed to volunteer in the church nursery.

Yawning, she jammed her hands in her coat pockets and sidestepped a group of guys coming out of the café. When her eyes locked with Weston's, she sucked in a breath. The people with him were laughing and talking over one another, so they didn't notice her until they'd almost bumped into her.

"Hey, look out." Weston grabbed the sleeve of the guy closest to him. "Watch where you're walking, man."

Conversation ground to a halt.

Blood roared behind her ears. "I thought you'd be long gone by now."

"Or still in jail," one of his friends mumbled.

The rest of the group chuckled.

"I wasn't in jail, my guy." Weston glared at them. "Go on, I'll meet you at the car in a minute. *Don't* leave without me."

Hayley tried not to smirk at that. It would be funny if they bailed and left him standing there in the cold. Except then she'd feel obligated to help him.

His friends meandered toward the parking lot, tossing mischievous glances over their shoulders.

"Listen." He held up both palms. "Before you unload on me, I want to admit right now that I had too much to drink."

"I'm aware. The officers who took our statements suspected as much."

The slurred words and unsteadiness had been solid clues as well, but she decided not to point out the obvious. He did look a little bit contrite.

"It was a rash decision to show up, and when I saw you dancing with him—obviously the big stars of the evening—I guess I just got super jealous."

"Why? We haven't dated in months."

Hurt flashed in Weston's brown eyes. "Which is why I've been trying to get you to talk to me. Then I saw a picture of you and that guy serving hot drinks together, so I had to do something.

Part of me hoped if I came to town and surprised you, you'd be all impressed that I made such a... such a—"

"Grand gesture?"

He kicked at a hard chunk of snow. "Is that what it's called?"

She nodded.

"Obviously I misread that."

"Obviously." She didn't want to be hurtful, but she couldn't let him think he had even the tiniest inkling of a second chance.

"Is your boyfriend okay?"

She hesitated. Probably not wise to clarify that Max wasn't her boyfriend. That might send a mixed message. "I haven't seen him today, but as far as I know, yes. You're fortunate that he didn't press charges, Weston. This could have ended poorly for you."

Weston heaved a defeated sigh. "Believe me, I know. I've heard all about it. My mom already called and chewed me out."

"Why in the world did you show up here unannounced?"

"It wasn't unannounced. I've texted you, liked and commented on your posts, but you never answered me."

"So you came anyway?"

He shrugged. "My friends wanted to see the northern lights, so I offered to bring them. When I got here, I heard some people at the hotel talking about how you and this guy with amnesia were a big deal. Then my friends and I started partying a little too hard and, well, you know what happened after that."

"There's still no excuse for punching someone in the face and saying horrible things."

He winced. "You're right. No excuse. I hope you can forgive me."

"I forgive you, but I just want to be super clear that you and I are over." She waved her hand between them. "There's zero chance we will get back together. We had some fun times, but I'm not interested. Or available."

A muscle twitched in his jaw. "Fair enough. Can I just say one more thing?"

She narrowed her gaze. "I feel like you've said plenty already."

"Please? It's important."

Sighing, she tipped her head back and sighed heavenward. "Fine. Hurry up, though. I'm running late."

"Are you sure he's who you want?"

Hayley gasped then glared at Weston. "Okay, we're done here."

"It's a valid question."

She brushed past him. "Goodbye, Weston."

"He broke your heart, remember?" Weston called after her. "He'll probably do it again if you let him."

Anger burned hot. Stupid Weston. Why had she

even bothered to speak to him? She hurried inside the café, then peeked through the door to make sure he hadn't followed her. He got in the back of a rented SUV. Snow sprayed behind the tires as the driver sped out of the parking lot. Hayley rubbed at the tightness in her chest. He might be out of sight, but she couldn't outrun his insensitive comments. And the part that bothered her the most was that he might be right.

Chapter Eleven

On Friday afternoon, Max trudged up the driveway, clutching a shovel. He tucked his chin and braced against the fierce wind howling around him. At least six inches of new snow had piled up since he'd come outside an hour ago. Clearing a path from the street to the garage for his dad's vehicle to park was futile. As soon as he shoveled a few feet, more snow filled in and then the wind blew it into drifts. Wet flakes clung to his lashes and he squinted, trying to see the front steps, so he could get out of the storm. He stashed the shovel under the porch, climbed the stairs and hurried inside.

Hayley turned from the window, arms crossed over her chest and concern etched on her face. "Are you all right?"

"I will be once I get warm." Shivering, he tugged off his soggy gloves and knit hat. "That wind is no joke."

Hayley tugged her green cardigan sweater tighter. "I'm glad Rachel is able to see a doctor in Anchorage for her follow-up instead of having to go all the way back to California, but this weather is nasty."

Max took off his jacket and hung it up nearby, then unlaced his winter boots. "My dad really wanted Rachel to take the baby along. I'm glad that didn't happen. A baby shouldn't be out in this weather."

"I don't think grown-ups should either," Hayley said. "The forecast predicted eighteen inches."

"So much for spring." Max set his boots near the heating vent to dry. "I'm glad Fiona's here, safe with us."

"Me too." She smiled. "I'm going to make some tea. Do you want anything?"

"Coffee, please." He peeked into the living room to check on Fiona. She sat buckled in her baby swing, swaying from side to side. A soothing rainforest sound played quietly from the speaker. Her eyes slowly closed.

What a cutie. He joined Hayley in the kitchen. "Do you know what time Rachel's appointment was scheduled for?"

Hayley lit the burner on the stove to heat the water in the kettle, then moved on to prepping the coffee maker to make a pot of the dark roast blend that Max had been drinking since he'd come home. "I think she said one thirty."

Max checked the time on the oven's clock. It was almost four fifteen now. "Dad told me he planned to drive home as soon as they were finished."

Hayley found her phone on the counter and glanced at the screen. "Your dad texted a few minutes ago. He's concerned about the high winds so they're going to get a hotel in Anchorage for the night."

"Really?" Max rubbed his fingertips along his chin. "I thought for sure he'd push through."

"His second message says that Rachel's anxious to get home, but if we could stay with Fiona tonight they would really appreciate it."

"Of course," Max said. "Do we have enough formula and diapers?"

Scrunching her nose, Hayley set her phone down. "Good question. Even though Juliet and I still help out almost every day, we're supposed to be letting Rachel increase her responsibilities in small steps each week, so we haven't kept up with the shopping."

"Makes sense." They probably had what they needed for the night, but if they got stuck here for a couple of days, it might get dicey.

He leaned against the counter. What did this mean for them? Alone with a baby in a snowstorm for the next several hours. Thoughts of snuggling on the couch in front of the roaring fire spun through his head. Pulse thrumming, he snuck a glance at Hayley. Sure, he wanted to kiss her. But he couldn't just tell her that. Could he? Did she want to kiss him?

Ever since the dance last weekend, he'd tried to engineer time alone with Hayley. Somehow, they always got interrupted or their schedules didn't align. He'd been 100 percent certain that she would've welcomed a kiss during their dance together, but he hadn't initiated because they hadn't been alone.

Then Weston showed up and ruined everything, which led to their emotional conversation in the community center kitchen. A conversation that still felt half-finished. Despite all the drama, she'd given him plenty of indications since he'd come home that she was interested. Sort of. She'd also done her best to keep him at arm's length.

He was certain something simmered between them. Something worth exploring. And now, standing in the kitchen, their eyes locked. Water gurgled through the coffee maker and the kettle whistled. He liked their proximity. Sure, he'd used his father and Rachel's plans as an excuse to ask questions, but he wasn't abandoning his mission to kiss Hayley. His eyes drifted to her lips.

"Max?"

"Mmm-hmm?"

"The coffee will be ready in a few minutes. Do you want to give Fiona her bottle?"

"I think she's already asleep."

"Will you check?"

Max hesitated, then turned and headed back to the living room. Sure enough, Fiona's eyes had closed. She had her little fist tucked under her chin. Definitely not interested in eating right now. He returned to the kitchen.

"She's out."

"All right." Hayley added a tea bag to her mug, then put the bottle of formula back in the fridge. "Do you want anything to eat?"

He shook his head. "Not right now, thanks. You?"

"No." She crossed to the pantry, opened the door and stepped inside. He wouldn't mind following her in there, but that seemed a little too aggressive. So he waited patiently. She stepped out holding a container of honey, then gave him a look. "Are you all right?"

He managed a nod.

"Are your memories coming back?"

"Not exactly."

She set the honey down and then took a spoon out of the drawer. Frowning, she cast him another glance. "Max, what's on your mind? You're acting a little cagey."

He crossed the kitchen in two quick strides. With his heart kicking against his ribs, he took the spoon from her hand and set it on the counter, then gently clasped her shoulders in his hands and turned her to face him.

"You," he whispered. "You're on my mind."

She gazed up at him, her eyes filled with a mixture of surprise and longing. "Max..."

He cradled her face in his hands. "Hayley, I want to kiss you. I've wanted to kiss you for days now. Is that all right?"

Hayley's fingers curled into the fabric of his shirt, pulling him closer.

This. This was what he'd been missing. All his frustrations about his lost memories vanished as he got lost in the depths of her green eyes.

Max's gaze flickered down to her lips before roaming her face again, silently asking for permission. Without a word, she closed the gap between them, her lips meeting his in a tender, tentative kiss. He tasted like mint gum and smelled like the fresh outdoors. His closeness made her head spin in the most delightful way. Then their kiss deepened, igniting a spark that had been smoldering between them for far too long.

It was a kiss that felt a little bit like a promise. A promise of something more to come. Time seemed to stand still as she leaned into his touch, the storm raging outside forgotten. Was this actually happening? Max was finally here with her, kissing her like he never wanted to let her go. His hands traveled from her cheeks to her hair, tangling in the soft locks as he pulled her closer. It was everything she had ever dreamed of.

As her heart swelled with affection, she conveniently shoved the past aside. All the time they spent apart had melted away and they were back to where they'd left off. The spicy scent of his aftershave, the stubble of his beard and the cocoon of his embrace made her tighten her hold on him.

Frankly, she didn't want this to end.

Despite her best efforts, she couldn't deny the intense feelings she had for him. She'd been determined to guard her heart, yet he had chipped away at her resistance. Only a few short months ago, she'd believed Max was gone forever. Now she wanted him in her arms and in her life. But what would happen when he decided to climb another mountain?

The pain of his rejection came roaring back.

Oh no. What had they done? Hayley broke the kiss and then pressed her hand to her mouth. Her skin hummed, and her thoughts were a jumbled mess.

Max kept his eyes closed just for a second before opening them and finding her gaze with his own. "What happened?"

His gravelly tone and flushed cheeks made him even more irresistible.

She was no match for his intense stare. She needed to gather her thoughts and put some distance between them, because she couldn't afford to get swept away in the moment.

"Nothing. Everything. I don't know." She scooted away from him and crossed the kitchen.

Reaching for the kettle, she poured hot water into her mug and steeped the tea bag. Then she pressed her palm against her chest to still her racing heart. Fiona's cries filtered in from the other room.

"That was a pretty incredible kiss. And now you seem like maybe you're not thrilled. Talk to me, Hayley. What's going on?"

She turned and faced him. "Well, for one, Fiona's crying."

He leaned against the counter with his arms crossed over his broad chest. "She's safe in her swing for a few minutes."

"We should really help her. Rachel doesn't like for her to cry very long."

"She's cried for more than five minutes before. Another minute or two won't hurt her. Hayley, please. What happened? Is it something I said? Something I did?"

She bit her thumbnail. "I don't know if this is a good idea. That kiss was incredible. You're incredible. It stirred up a lot of emotions for me, though. I wasn't expecting it." She fidgeted with her mug, avoiding his intense gaze. "I've been trying to guard my heart, Max. But being with you today, seeing how good we are together...it's making it really hard. I'm not sure I can do this."

Pain flashed in his eyes. "Do what?"

"Jump-start a relationship with you when you still have a long way to go in your recovery."

He glanced down at his feet. "My ankle feels fine."

"I don't mean just your ankle. I mean…all of you." She gestured up and down in the air.

Max's brows sailed upward.

Oh, she was not handling this well at all.

"Do you think I'm damaged goods?" His voice was low, but there was an edge to it.

"No!" She shook her head. "No, of course not. That's not what I meant."

"Then what do you mean?"

"What happens when you decide to climb another mountain? What happens when you leave?"

Max's expression turned serious as he studied her face. "I won't deny that climbing will always be a huge part of my life. But so are you. I want us to work through our issues together."

Hayley's heart swelled at his words, but she couldn't shake off the fear that still lingered in the back of her mind. "Can we really do that?"

Max ran his hand through his tousled hair. "The neurologist I saw this week said it's possible I won't ever remember my past. I'll have to learn to move forward, accepting those gaps will always be there. The question is will you be able to move forward?"

His words stung. How could he put this back on her? She wanted to believe that she could move forward, but now she wasn't so sure.

"It's not just the memory loss, Max." She bit

her lip, trying to tamp down the emotion welling in her throat. "I told you that you hurt me when you shut me out and left town."

"And I told you that I want to make things right." His eyes darkened. "Why won't you give us a second chance?"

"It's not that simple," she whispered. Hot tears stung her eyes. "I—I need time to think. Right now I'm going to go help Fiona."

She hurried into the living room. What a mess. Why had she allowed herself to get into this situation? Yeah, okay, so she'd wanted to kiss him. On more than one occasion. But now that they had, she regretted complicating their...well, everything.

She'd been so sure she was done with him. After all the heartache and pain, she had finally moved on. But then he came back into her life, winning her over with his charm and making her believe her dreams were actually achievable. That kiss confirmed how she truly felt, but at the same time, she was terrified of being hurt. How could she trust that he wouldn't leave her once more? And if he did, how would she ever recover from losing him again?

Hard work would help him sort this out. That and prayer. He'd tossed and turned for the past two nights, asking the Lord for guidance and replaying his conversation with Hayley. And of course, he'd replayed that amazing kiss more than once.

His face heated, just thinking about how much he'd enjoyed holding Hayley in his arms. Till it had all gone south, and she'd gotten upset.

"Max, help me load in more Sheetrock, please." Tim, one of the guys on the work crew at the clinic, tugged on a pair of gloves.

"Sure, no problem," Max said, although he hated to leave the warmth of the construction site. The space heater glowed orange in the corner, and classic rock streamed from a paint splattered speaker resting on top of a box of new light fixtures.

Friday's storm had blown through and left behind twenty-five below zero temperatures plus two feet of snow, which the howling wind had shoved into high drifts around town. That was April in Alaska for you. He put on his coat, gloves and his knit hat, then followed Jason outside.

The freezing air stung his cheeks and snow crunched under his boots as they hurried toward the truck idling at the curb. It took two trips, but they made short work of hauling the Sheetrock into the building, carefully leaning it against the wall.

Dust floating in the air, combined with the smell of mud and tape they used for the project sparked a memory. Max paused, his coat halfway unzipped. He drew in another deep breath. More of the memory unfolded. He closed his eyes. They were on a large lot in a small town in Alaska. It was the summer after his first year in college, and he'd been hired to work on the construction crew. They were building a house for a family who'd lost everything in a fire. Mosquitoes buzzed and the sun on his already sunburned neck made him wish he'd packed sunscreen. Long hours made his muscles ache. It had all been worth it, though, when they'd finished the house and the family had moved in.

Max opened his eyes, took off his coat then sat down on a workbench near the door.

Tim eyed him. "You okay, man?"

"Yeah." He shoved back his hat and scratched his head. "Just had a memory come back, that's all."

"Cool." Tim grinned. "Hope you remembered something good."

"It wasn't bad." Max took off his hat and gave his head a quick shake. "It's weird how my brain does that."

"When you're ready, let's start hanging drywall in this bathroom." Tim gestured over his shoulder with his thumb. "If we hustle, we can probably have it finished by tomorrow."

Max nodded and pushed to his feet. Before he could put on his tool belt Garrett came in.

"Hey, sorry to interrupt. Max, have you heard from Hayley today?"

His stomach sank. "No. Why?"

"She didn't show up for work and she's not answering her phone. I know you're busy in here, but would you mind going by her place and checking in on her? We're short-staffed as it is, and I really can't spare anybody. It's not like her to do this though."

Max glanced at Tim. "I'll be back. Can I bring you coffee to make up for it?"

"You sure can. Large white chocolate mocha, extra whip. And don't forget the sprinkles."

"Got it." Max checked to make sure he had his keys and his phone. Thankfully, someone at the DMV had taken pity on him and fast-tracked a new license. With access to one of his dad's extra vehicles, he had the freedom to move about town without having to rely on anyone for transportation. One more step in the right direction.

Out in the parking lot, a man hailed him down. "Hey, Max."

Max slowed his steps. The guy wasn't someone he recognized, but he was starting to get used to strangers approaching him like they were old friends.

"Hey, I'm Cody." The guy standing near the front of his large truck looked to be around fifty years old. He wore a sling on his right arm, and his breath left white puffs in the morning air. "I'm starting physical therapy on my rotator cuff tear, but I wanted to talk to you about joining an expedition to Denali in May."

Max glanced at his arm. "Um, maybe?"

"Yeah, yeah," Cody chuckled. "I know, this isn't a good look for me, but I'm optimistic that it's all going to be okay. Are you interested? My boys and I have started working out three evenings a week at a warehouse out on Fairview Road. You're welcome to join us."

"I know the place," Max said. "Let me get your number. Maybe you can text me the details."

"Sure." Cody rattled off his number.

Max quickly put his contact info into his phone. "I'm definitely interested. Thanks for the invitation. I'll be in touch."

Cody gave him a friendly nod. "Sounds good."

Max climbed in his truck, started the engine, then sent Cody a quick text so they could touch base later. As he gazed through the windshield at Denali's towering form half-shrouded in billowing clouds, a mix of excitement and fear swirled in his gut. He was determined to conquer the mountain, but doubts crept into his mind. Was he really ready for this? Would he be able to handle it?

He gritted his teeth, then shifted the truck into gear. The neurologist had reviewed the report from Max's CT scan and cleared him to resume all activities. He'd even said it might be beneficial for Max to climb again. So now he had zero excuses. His past and his memory loss couldn't hold him hostage forever. He had to get back on that mountain, no matter the cost.

Max drove slowly behind a plow clearing the

road leading to Hayley's neighborhood. Thoughts of her weighed on his mind. Garrett was right. Not showing up for work and ignoring her phone wasn't like her at all.

When he arrived in front of the small Craftsman-style house she shared with Juliet, he spotted her car parked in the driveway. No recent tire tracks though, and an unusual stillness surrounding the place.

He parked beside the curb, then strode up the driveway and knocked on the front door. But there was no answer. Concern gnawed at him as he tried the handle and found it locked. Had she stayed at her parents' house instead? He pressed up on his tiptoes and tried peering into the small rectangular window on the maroon door for any sign of movement inside. Nothing. So weird. He tried calling Hayley's phone again, but it went straight to voicemail. Then he sent Juliet and Rachel a text asking when they'd last seen or heard from Hayley. Getting Tim's coffee and hanging drywall would have to wait. He had to make sure she was okay.

Chapter Twelve

Her whole body hurt. She hadn't felt this terrible since she'd caught an edge with her snowboard and tumbled down the hill at Winterhaven last year. She needed to get out of bed and grab the extra quilt from the linen closet in the hallway, but she didn't have the energy.

Her head throbbed. Even her eyeballs ached. Teeth chattering, she curled into a tight ball. How could she feel so cold yet so hot at the same time? This had to be the flu. Annabelle had been complaining of a sore throat at work last week. Hayley had tried to ignore her own scratchy throat after church yesterday, blaming it on fatigue. Garrett's entire family was sick last week as well. This timing was the worst. She had a meeting with an architect about plans for the recreational venue, not to mention nine patients on her schedule today. Who would cover those if more of her coworkers were sick, too? But her biggest concern was spreading germs to Fiona. She'd held her quite a bit on Friday and part of Saturday until the Butlers finally got home. What happened to a tiny little thing like her if she got a high fever? That would be an emergency for sure.

She squinted into the darkness. The blue glow from the night-light plugged in to the wall did little to offer any help. Where was her phone? She fumbled on the nightstand. Nope. Had it fallen? She patted her hand underneath the covers. Maybe she dropped it last night when she'd been mindlessly scrolling, unable to fall asleep, thanks to her almost constant thoughts about Max. What was she going to do? She tried to think, but her brain felt like it was packed with mud.

She had to get in touch with Rachel and warn her that Fiona had likely been exposed to a contagious virus. What did Max have on his schedule today? They'd barely spoken after their epic kitchen kiss. Mostly because she'd avoided him. But this was nearly an emergency. He'd likely respond to her text if she reached out. If she could find her phone. In a minute, she'd get up and go look downstairs. Groaning, she tugged the covers up to her chin to ward off the chill.

The muffled sound of someone knocking, then ringing her doorbell, forced her to open her eyes. Whoever that was, she needed them. Wincing, she pushed back the covers slowly then tried to sit up. Her brain felt like it was caught in a vise grip. She immediately laid back down. What was she going to do? This was the worst. It took all her strength to yank the covers back up to her chin. Another wave of chills racked her body.

"Lord, please help. Send someone soon," she whispered.

A few minutes later, footsteps thumped on the stairs.

"Hayley?" Max's voice came through her closed bedroom door. "Are you in there?"

"Oh, thank You, Lord." She forced herself to sit up again. "Come in."

The door opened a crack and Max peeked in. "Are you all right?"

"No," she croaked. "I'm super sick."

Max nudged the door wide.

"Wait." She held up her hand. "Don't come any closer. You don't want this."

A smile tugged at one corner of his mouth as he turned on a small lamp on her dresser. "It's probably too late for that."

Oh. Thoughts of their kiss spooled through her muddled brain. She admired his ruddy cheeks and clean-shaven jaw. Under his coat, he wore the dark red and navy blue plaid flannel button-down over a navy blue shirt that she liked so much. His faded jeans were speckled with drywall dust.

"I'm so sorry. I hear it's going around town. What can I do?"

She squeezed her eyes shut. "Can you find my phone? I need to let Rachel know that Fiona might be at risk of catching this."

Max's phone chimed. His jacket rustled. "This message is from Juliet. She was on her way to help Rachel with Fiona, but she didn't feel good, so she went to your parents' place instead. Her fever is high so she's going to sequester herself in your old bedroom."

"Oh no." Hayley groaned. "We're dropping like flies. You'd better get out of here."

"I'm not going anywhere until you have what you need."

Hayley opened her eyes. He hovered near the end of her bed, frowning at his phone. "What about Fiona?"

Max pocketed his phone. "I'll make sure Fiona is okay. First, I'm bringing you some medicine, soda and crackers."

"And my phone? Please? It's probably downstairs on the counter."

"Coming right up." He offered a smile so tender she thought she might burst into tears.

"I'm going to take care of you, Hayley. If you'll let me."

Her heart pinched. A tear trickled from the corner of her eye.

"Hey, hey." Concern flashed in his eyes as he sank to his knees beside her bed. "Why are you crying?"

"No, don't come any closer, Max. You can't afford to get sick either."

"Just tell me why you're crying, then I'll go and get your stuff."

She sniffed. "I'm disappointed with myself, that's all."

"This isn't your fault. People get sick."

Hayley took the tissue he offered from the box nearby. "But I have so much to do."

"Everything will work out. You need to rest and focus on getting well. I'll be back in a few minutes."

"Thank you."

"Anything else?"

She shook her head.

"I've got this." He gently squeezed her arm. "Don't worry."

But she did worry. That was kind of her thing. If she didn't worry and keep taking care of everyone, then who would?

Hayley was right. They were dropping like flies.

Max exited his truck in his family's driveway, then jogged toward the front door. After taking care of Hayley, he'd received a text from Rachel asking him to come by. She had chills and a high fever as well. His father had left early this morning for his flight out of Anchorage. He paused on the steps and sent a quick text to Tim and Garrett, explaining the situation and letting them know he wouldn't be back today.

Jason would have to get his own mocha.

As soon as he stepped inside, he heard Fiona crying in her nursery. Poor thing. He quickly took off his boots and his coat, then hurried upstairs. Rachel's bedroom door was closed. Max paused in the hallway outside Fiona's room and whispered a prayer for patience and wisdom. Sure, he'd taken care of her for an hour or two here and there, but someone had always been close by if he needed backup. Even though his dad clearly wasn't great with babies, together they'd managed to keep Fiona mostly content and fed during their dinner out together several weeks ago.

He'd learned a lot about his baby sister's needs and preferences, and could soothe her crying when others couldn't. Still, it had felt like a team effort. Now with Hayley, Juliet and Rachel all feeling sick, he'd have to do what he could on his own. What would he do if he started feeling bad? He'd never neglect Fiona, but he wasn't confident he'd be able to care for her if he wasn't well.

He blew out a long breath. He didn't have another option at the moment, so he turned the knob and pushed the door open.

"Oh my." The rank odor that greeted him made him take a step back. He tugged his shirt collar over his nose and forced himself to move toward the crib. "Fiona, my girl, what is up?"

She lay in her crib on her back. Rachel had put her in one of those warm, zippered sleep sack things. Fiona's face was red, her hair damp and she smelled terrible.

Max looked around the nursery. What to do? She'd probably been crying for a while, so he couldn't let her just lay there. But, man, she was a mess. Did he need to give her a bath? How was he supposed to do that?

"All right, first things first. Let's survey the damage." He let go of his shirt, grimaced, then lifted her from the crib and carried her to the changing table. A pacifier sat on the wood surface.

"Here, try this." He offered it to her, but she turned her head away and screamed louder.

"Okay, okay, shh." He gently swept her damp hair off her forehead. Tears trickled from the corners of her eyes and clung to her lashes. "I know, I know. You're mad and you have every right to be. But I'm here, and even though I'm not much help, I'm all you've got so let's figure this out, okay?"

He got her out of her soiled clothes and the offensive diaper. Then he wrapped her in a blanket and carried her down the hall to the bathroom. Thankfully, whoever had bathed her last had left the supplies he needed in easy access. A few minutes later, he had her mostly cleaned up. She was not at all content, but at least she wasn't filthy. Maybe it was just wishful thinking on his part, but she seemed to be crying slightly less.

"See? That wasn't so bad, was it?" He wrapped her in a clean pink towel with an elephant's face on the hood. Then he grabbed a diaper on his way past her nursery and headed downstairs. She was gnawing on her little fist now, a sign he'd learned meant hunger.

"All right, one thing at a time." He nestled her in the crook of his elbow and peeked inside the refrigerator. One bottle of mixed formula waited for them. "Score, you've got breakfast waiting for you, kiddo. Let's make it warm."

He put the bottle in the warmer and carried Fiona into the front room.

"I wish your mom wasn't sick. Spending your Monday with me is probably not what you had in mind." He plucked a clean pair of pajamas and a white onesie off the pile waiting in the plastic laundry bin. He put her diaper on, then the clean clothes. It wasn't as challenging as the first time he'd done it. She screamed at him the whole time, though.

"I know, I know. I'm doing the best I can. You're being a real champ about all of this."

Man, this was a workout. He scooped her up, snagged the towel and hung it on the kitchen chair and then retrieved the warm bottle. Back in the living room, he settled into a corner of the sofa and offered her the formula. She wolfed it down like she hadn't eaten in days.

"There you go. How about that? You're clean, dry and you're eating. Life is good, right?"

She stared up at him and made contented noises while she drank.

"You're doing great, sweetheart. Now, here's the thing. We have to figure out what to do for Hayley. I know you're focused on your own needs right now, and that's fine. Totally valid. But we need to get her well and keep other people from getting sick. Any tips?"

Her smooth brow furrowed as she kept drinking.

"Nothing yet, huh? That's fine. I'll brainstorm. You just stay focused on breakfast."

He breathed deep, inhaling her clean baby scent and let himself enjoy the moment. She was so precious. Even though he wasn't thrilled that he didn't have his memories back, taking care of her had been an unexpected blessing. Well, most of the time.

"See? Big brother knows what to do. I can step up in a pinch. Now, as soon as Hayley feels better, how can I convince her I'm reliable and trustworthy?"

That was the big question that spooled through his head. If he wanted to win her heart, somehow he'd have to prove to her, through his actions and not only his words, that he wasn't going to break her heart. Or let her suffer alone.

She'd done so much for everyone else. Now seemed like the ideal time to care for her. Yeah, okay, so it was bad news that she'd gotten sick. Now that she'd been forced to take it easy, he'd have to be the one showing up for her. Providing for her needs and helping her get well.

* * *

Two days. Hayley rubbed sleep from her eyes, blinked, then checked her phone again. She'd been in this bed for two days. Well, mostly. Other than her groggy, fever-induced stumbles to the bathroom. She couldn't remember going downstairs at all. She did have faint memories of Max hovering at her bedside, checking in and dropping off more supplies. She glanced at the nightstand. A half-full glass of water sat waiting for her, and she quickly drank it down. Empty wrappers indicated that she had taken whatever over-the-counter medicine he'd left for her.

Oh, Max. What a sweet guy. Who knew she'd have to depend on him to get her through a nasty bout of the flu?

She pushed back the covers and swung her legs over the side of the bed. Instantly, she felt lightheaded. But she wasn't lying back down. She had to get up. She couldn't afford to spend any more time away from her busy life. Who had seen her patients this week? And the architect?

"Oh, no." She groaned. Ever since she'd been awarded the grant and she and Jack had hammered out an agreement for her to lease the land, she'd been so pumped to move forward with the rec center plans. But now she'd blown off the meeting. Had he come to town for nothing? She grabbed her phone and scrolled through her text messages. Surprisingly, very few people had reached out. Huh. That was weird. She scrolled down a little farther.

Uh-oh. This nasty virus had infected her sisters and her parents. Seemed like Max and maybe her brother Wyatt were the only two who were still healthy.

She rubbed her face and yawned, wondering if poor Fiona had gotten sick too. Who was looking out for her? She set the empty glass on the nightstand and forced herself to get up. Her legs felt like limp spaghetti noodles. She walked slowly across the room and stepped out into the hallway. An appealing scent of something comforting and familiar wafted up the stairs. She turned back, grabbed her fluffy robe from the hook behind the door and slipped it on. Juliet must be home. At least one of them was feeling well. She cinched the belt at the waist. Thankfully, she didn't have the chills anymore either. That was good.

She slowly worked her way down the stairs one step at a time, gripping the handrail tightly. The middle stair creaked. Max looked up from where he stood next to her sofa, folding a load of towels.

"Hi." He grinned. "You're awake."

She nodded then looked around. A vanilla-scented candle sat in the middle of her clean kitchen counter, its golden flame flickering. "What's going on? What are you doing here?"

His smile dimmed. "I almost scooped you up

and hauled you to the ER. Your fever stayed at 102 degrees for a day and a half."

"When did you check my temperature?"

Max snapped the clean white towel before folding it.

"I checked your temperature three or four times. You don't remember?"

Hayley yawned, then stretched her arms overhead. "Nope. Thanks for looking out for me. How's Fiona?"

"She is her usual feisty self. No fever yet."

"Who's been watching her?"

"Me. My dad's home now though, and Rachel seems to be feeling better." Max set the stack of towels on the back of the sofa, then crossed to the kitchen. He lifted a lid on a pot sitting on the front burner. The aroma of chicken filled the air. He had fixed something to eat too? What in the world?

She walked the rest of the way down the stairs. "And you've stayed well?"

"So far, so good." Max opened the oven door and peered inside. Then he closed it and adjusted the timer on the microwave. "Guess what? Not only is Fiona healthy, she's been sleeping through the night."

Hayley clapped her hands. "That's amazing. I'm so proud of her." Her stomach rumbled. "Something smells good. What are you making?"

"Someone from church brought you a couple of meals. I put one in the freezer because I didn't know if you'd feel like eating yet. Right now I'm reheating the chicken noodle soup and warming some dinner rolls."

"Where'd you find that candle?"

"It was in your hall closet. Hope you don't mind. I was just about to vacuum but didn't want to wake you."

"Max." She grinned at him. "This is amazing. Wow. Why did you do all of this?"

He met her gaze and held it. "Because I care about you, Hayley, and I want to help. Do you want something to drink?"

"I'll stick with ginger ale, please." She crossed the kitchen and sat down at her small round kitchen table near the window.

"Crackers?" He held up a package.

She nodded.

He brought her the cold soda, a cup of ice and the crackers.

"Have you been taking care of Fiona by yourself for the past two days?"

"Yep." He winked. "And I took care of you too."

Warmth heated her cheeks. "Thank you. For everything. I don't know what I would've done without you, especially since it sounds like everyone in my family is sick too."

"You're welcome." He claimed the chair across from hers. "Juliet is bouncing back, but she's staying with Savannah to help with her kids."

"Oh my. This must be super contagious." She

opened the can of soda and poured it over the ice. "I appreciate your help, and I'm really glad to hear that Fiona's not sick. A baby with a high fever could be disastrous."

"She's a champ."

A popular country music song streamed from the portable speaker on the counter beside Max's phone. Her place was so clean, it smelled good and he'd made sure she had something to eat. What a kind and thoughtful guy. And she did love the comforting aroma of soup simmering on the stove and fresh rolls warming in the oven. A girl could get used to this kind of pampering.

Oh brother. This fever must have messed with her head. She reached for a cracker. Yeah, okay, so she'd meant it when she said she was grateful that he stepped up. Not every guy would risk getting sick to meet the needs of others. Sitting here, just the two of them, offered her a glimpse of a life with the things she'd dreamed of for so long—faith. Family. Security.

But the doubt instantly crept in. He might have done the right thing this time. What about the next time he wanted to summit a treacherous peak in a faraway place? Was she supposed to just give him her blessing and hope for the best?

Chapter Thirteen

Max stood alone in the guesthouse, scrolling through Cody's recommended packing list. He'd prepared for this trek up Denali with meticulous attention to detail. Except one task remained that he'd conveniently avoided: breaking the news to Hayley.

His stomach tightened. She was not going to be happy.

He closed his pack with a satisfying zip, then hoisted his gear onto his back to test the weight. Things had been off between them for a few weeks. The memory of their wonderful kiss during the snowstorm lingered in his mind, making it hard to focus on anything else. But then the flu had hit Opportunity, disrupting their budding romance and forcing them to put things on hold. He had done everything he could to take care of her, cleaning her place and cooking dinner, hoping to show her how much she meant to him. But somehow, things hadn't turned out the way he had hoped.

Yeah, okay, so she'd been appreciative. When he caught her smiling at him a few times, he couldn't help but feel a spark between them. But her guarded expression hinted at something deeper that he couldn't quite decipher. Was he just a friend to her, or did their spontaneous kiss hold more meaning? The uncertainty dogged him, making it hard to fully relax around her.

So he was following through on his plans to climb Denali with Cody and his sons. They'd trained together for several weeks. Max had zero reservations about joining their expedition. Regardless of how Hayley reacted when he told her, he wasn't changing his mind. He had to do this.

He took a lap around the guesthouse, clutching the straps on the pack with both hands. Climbing Denali with this group of guys was his chance to prove to himself, and to everyone, really, that he could conquer this challenge and vanquish his fears. Yes, it was possible that there would be a climbing accident, but he'd spent several hours with these guys already. They'd mapped out an emergency plan, chosen their best route toward the summit, and Cody insisted their guide was one of the best around. The weather forecast looked decent. He knew this wasn't the recipe for suddenly getting his memories back, but frankly, he was tired of sitting around waiting for his brain to kick into gear.

Because what was the point of staying home

and avoiding danger? What if playing it safe never brought back the chunks of his past that he couldn't recall? He put the pack down, leaned it against the sofa and cleaned up the discarded packaging from the items he'd purchased at the sporting goods store. He'd have to focus on the present. Take one step at a time. If they got to base camp and things didn't look good, they could always overnight and wait out any surprise storms.

Someone knocked at the door. He looked out the window. Hayley stood on the steps.

He took a deep breath, mentally preparing himself for the conversation he was about to have. He had to tell her.

After he'd finished painting a wall at the clinic yesterday, she'd popped in to check out the progress. If they stayed on schedule, the expansion would be ready in about a week. Max had tried to bring up the topic of his climb, but he couldn't find the right words. Now there was no more time for delay.

When he opened the door, she greeted him with a bright smile. His pulse sped at the sight of her. She looked beautiful, as always, with her long auburn hair cascading over her shoulders and her stunning green eyes roaming his face. He longed to pull her into his arms and re-create the magic of that kiss.

No. He couldn't. That wasn't right.

He forced a smile. "Hey."

She cocked her head to the side. "Is everything okay? You seem nervous."

Max hesitated, then stepped back. "Come on in. I need to talk to you about something."

Hayley followed him inside. After he closed the door, she reached for his hand. "Whatever it is, you can tell me," she said softly.

He squeezed her hand before pulling away. "It's about Denali."

She froze. "What about it?"

"I'm going." His words came out in a rush. "I'm going to be climbing Denali with Cody and his sons. We leave tomorrow."

She couldn't believe what she was hearing.

"Are you kidding me?" Hayley planted her hands on her hips and glared at Max. "You mean you're just going for a hike, right?"

He'd just uttered the words she never wanted to hear. It seemed like a cruel joke. But when she met Max's steady gaze, there was no hint of playfulness or deception in his expression. He was serious. Max's forehead wrinkled. His strong features were etched with determination as he spoke.

"I'm doing exactly what I said I'd do. What I've been saying I'll do since that first day Garrett evaluated my ankle injury. The neurologist cleared me to climb, and Garrett said my ankle is great. Cody and his sons have poured their hearts and souls into this dream, and I'm pumped that I get to be a part of their journey."

Hayley's heart stuttered. The memory of his previous attempt to climb dredged up all her old heartache. Sure, he'd been in another country, but that treacherous climb had nearly cost him his life. They'd spent weeks awaiting news of his rescue. Eventually they'd been forced to accept that he hadn't survived. "How can you possibly do this? It's the very thing that nearly got you killed."

"Which is exactly why I should get back out there, right? I can't let fear of failure influence my choices."

"How about fear of death? How about fear of another traumatic brain injury? What if you fall again?"

His expression hardened. "Thanks for that vote of confidence, Hayley. What if I summit the mountain and have the most incredible experience of my life? Haven't I taken multiple trips to Denali?"

"Yes. Of course you have. So wouldn't that be a perfect reason to not? You've already done it."

"But I don't remember. What if this climb triggers my memories?"

He seemed more determined than ever to make this climb. She dug her fingernails into her palms. Wasn't there anything she could say to reason with him? "What if it doesn't and you get hurt?"

He blew out a long breath and then raked his

hand through his hair. "I know there are risks involved. But I can't keep living my life in fear of the unknown. And I don't understand why you're challenging me on this."

"And I don't understand why you can't see my point of view." She hesitated, then said, "I care about you, Max. Your family cares about you. Why would you put yourself in harm's way like this again, especially after all you've been through?"

He turned and stared at her. The silence between them felt heavy. Weighted down by their unspoken words. "I told you, I can't let my fear win. I was born to be a climber."

She scoffed, no longer able to conceal her doubt. "Have you considered that maybe you were born for something else? To build houses or drive heavy equipment, or maybe teach school. How do you know that summiting Denali is what you're supposed to do next?"

He hesitated. "I don't know for sure, but I do know that staying home and letting fear hold me back won't get me anywhere."

"No one will think you're a coward if you don't do this, Max."

"I will. I'll think I'm a coward. And that matters."

"You know what?" Anger roiled inside her. "There's evidently nothing I can say to convince you not to do this. So go ahead. Leave. Risk your life. What I think doesn't matter."

"Hayley, wait."

She stomped out the door and slammed it behind her. Birds chirped and the spring sunshine spilled across the path toward the main house. She hurried to her car, half-wishing he'd come after her. When he didn't, she started to sob. After all the time they'd spent together, that romantic kiss, and how far he'd come in his healing process since he'd been back in Opportunity, why couldn't he recognize that he was putting all of his progress in jeopardy? Why didn't her fear matter? Once again, her feelings were irrelevant. Max wasn't willing to think about anybody other than himself. Why had she been so foolish to think that this time something might have changed?

Guilt nagged at her as she started the car and drove away. Had she been too harsh? Lashing out like that? She sniffled, then swiped at her tears with the cuff of her shirtsleeve. Maybe he didn't truly remember his previous climbs, or the danger that potentially lurked on Denali's perilous mountainside. Since he had no memories, maybe it was too alluring for him to resist. Like climbing for the first time. Still, that didn't change the fact that this expedition could be dangerous for someone who had already experienced a near-death accident. And she couldn't stand the thought of losing him again.

"Buddy, we've got to hunker down and ride this thing out. We're going to be fine." Max's voice wavered as he tried to sound confident, but even he wasn't sure if he believed his own words. He glanced at Cody, who sat in their tent, pale and sweating, his leg propped up on a stack of duffel bags. The makeshift splint around his compound lower leg fracture wasn't enough, but it was the best they could do for now.

Cody groaned. "I can't believe this is happening. I just recovered from my rotator cuff thing, and now this."

"Doctors can fix broken legs..." Max reminded him then trailed off. He stared at the frozen condensation on the inside of the tent. The wind shrieked outside like a wild animal, making the walls ripple. He tightened his sleeping bag around himself then squeezed a handwarmer between his palms, trying to keep warm.

"Your optimism isn't helping much, you know," Cody said, his voice hoarse.

"Maybe not," Max admitted. "But it's all we've got. I'm choosing to believe a chopper will come as soon as it's safe. They said they'd get here, but this weather..." He stopped short of verbalizing his fears of an avalanche. Instead, he pulled out his phone again. No service. Of course. "Rex and TJ hailed a dispatcher on the satellite phone this morning. They'll get word to the right people on the ground. As soon as someone knows exactly where we are—"

Max paused, frowning as a vague, slippery

thought tickled the edge of his memory. What was it? Something important. He shook his head.

"Never mind." He shoved the phone back into his pocket.

Cody watched him, concern etched into his face. "What's going on with you, Max? Are you in shock? You've been zoning out all day."

Max didn't answer right away. He leaned back, closing his eyes, and began to breathe deeply, as he'd been taught. Inhale for four. Hold for four. Exhale for four. His chest rose and fell as he fought back the panic threatening to flood his mind. The memories were there—just out of reach, like shadows slipping through his fingers.

He whispered a prayer under his breath. "Please, Lord. Help me remember. I know this is important. Not just for my sake, but for Hayley's, too."

Her face flashed in his mind, clearer than it had been in days. Hayley crying. Distraught. Her cheeks blotchy and streaked with tears that clung to her lashes.

You're crushing my dreams, Max, she'd said, her voice shaking. *You're running away because your family is falling apart, and you're picking a mountain in another country over a relationship with me. How could you? How could you be so selfish?*

The memory hit him like a blow to the chest. He groaned, the sound low and guttural.

Cody sat up slightly, grimacing from the movement. "What's wrong? Do you need Rex or TJ?"

Cody's sons were safe in a tent nearby with their guide, who evidently had sustained a concussion. "One of my memories, a big one, just came back," Max said, his voice barely audible. He rubbed his aching temples. "I'm starting to understand why Hayley has been so standoffish."

Cody's bushy gray eyebrows furrowed. "You were in a relationship with her before?"

Max nodded, his throat tight. "She was furious when I told her I was going on this expedition. I thought she was being dramatic, but now…now I see why."

"And how do you feel about her?"

Max hesitated. "I love her." The words felt like a release, but they also carried the weight of regret. "I want us to be together, but she's resisted at every turn." Well, minus their kiss. He swallowed hard, keeping that detail to himself. "She deserves better than what I've given her. I ran away when life got hard. And now, here I am, stuck on a mountain while she's probably figuring out how to move on without me."

Cody sighed, shifting to find a less painful position. "Well, like you said, the best thing we can do for her—and everyone else who cares about us—is to hunker down, ride this out and get out of here alive."

Max nodded, although Cody paraphrasing

Max's own words offered little comfort. He closed his eyes again, straining to pull more memories to the surface. But the moment had passed, like the wind blowing fog in.

It didn't matter. He finally recalled the one crucial detail that had eluded him for so long: Hayley had begged him not to go. She'd pleaded with him to choose her, to prioritize their future together. And he hadn't.

Max swallowed hard, his chest tightening. "I messed up," he whispered, mostly to himself.

Cody didn't respond. Max stared at the tent walls trembling in the storm. All he could do now was pray—pray for a second chance to keep his word, to make things right with Hayley, and to prove he wasn't the selfish man she'd believed him to be.

Outside, the wind screamed, drowning out his whispered plea.

Chapter Fourteen

"I understand why you're worried, and you have every right to tell Max how you feel," Savannah said gently, adding a bunch of red grapes to the middle of her charcuterie board. "But he does have to make his own choices."

"I know," Hayley said, her voice tight. "I hear what you're saying, but it was like he didn't even care that I was worried."

"I doubt that's true, sweetheart," Mom said, carefully shaking whole wheat crackers from a box onto the edge of the board.

Juliet added several small slices of sharp cheddar.

Hayley had gathered with her mom and sisters while Dad and Wyatt were off on a fishing adventure. Since Jack was on a long flight overseas, they'd invited Rachel and Fiona to join them. After recovering from the flu, they'd all agreed they were overdue for a relaxing evening of girl time.

Not that Hayley could relax fully, knowing Max was probably roped off on the side of a massive cliff somewhere.

"At least he's not alone, right?" Savannah asked, her tone hopeful.

"No, he's not going as a guide. He's with another group. But it's still dangerous."

"Lots of people climb Denali and come home without anything going wrong," Mom said.

"I know, but this is the same thing that caused his serious injury before. His memories still haven't returned. Doesn't that mean his brain hasn't healed? So why would he risk another injury so soon?"

When everyone had a cold drink and plates loaded with meats, cheeses, crackers, nuts and grapes, they gathered around the long table in the Morgans' dining room. Mom cradled Fiona in her arms while Rachel set up a portable high chair nearby.

"Is it possible," Mom asked gently, "that Max still doesn't know how you feel about him? That maybe this tension between you has confused him?"

Hayley shifted in her chair. She wasn't ready to share the details about their epic snowstorm kiss. "We've tried talking about our issues a couple of times. He doesn't really get it. And he still hasn't recovered his memories, so I'm starting to wonder if he'll ever understand me."

Silence filled the room, broken only by the clinking of silverware and Fiona's soft babbling.

"So maybe," Savannah said, "this is really

about your fear of rejection and not so much about Max climbing again."

Hayley couldn't mask her irritation. "Isn't fear of rejection a legitimate concern?"

"Except Max has never been shy about who he is," Juliet said. "You know he's going to climb something, hike something, jump over something. That's who he is. You're not going to keep him safe at home forever. He's an outdoorsman. Besides, wasn't the idea to send him to places he'd been before to maybe trigger a memory?"

Hayley let out a long breath and took a generous bite of chocolate Rachel had brought. The creamy filling exploded on her taste buds. She swallowed and immediately reached for a second piece.

"So, you guys think I'm in the wrong here?"

Her sisters exchanged glances.

"Not wrong," Mom said. "Maybe just a little off in your delivery."

"Nothing wrong with telling him you're worried," Savannah added. "But if he doesn't know why you're worried, maybe it's time for a follow-up conversation."

"I don't know how many different ways I can tell him that he crushed me when he left."

"Oh, dear." Juliet gave her an empathetic look. "Don't you think it's time to be honest with him about how much you genuinely care about him? He's been through a lot. Even if he never gets his memories back, he understands what it's like to need a second chance."

"I don't know. I mean, yes, you're right. I should." Hayley took a long sip of her ice water. "I keep thinking about what you said because he basically told me the same thing before he left. Adventure will always be in him. So how can I cope with that?"

"You seemed fine with it before."

"He hadn't hurt himself before." She sighed. "I'm letting my fear get the best of me. But... I need him to choose me."

"He can choose you and still love the outdoors," Juliet said. "You're holding him accountable for something he doesn't even know he did. That hardly seems fair."

"Expecting me to overlook my hurt is equally unfair!" Hayley protested.

Juliet opened her mouth to respond, but her phone chimed. She glanced at the screen, her features turning pale.

"Uh-oh."

"What? What's going on?"

"That was a text from Jasper and Levi. There's a search party going up the mountain. Climbers are stranded at base camp. Someone's injured. There's a terrible storm."

"No." Hayley's stomach bottomed out. "Please, no. It can't be."

"Can I say something?" Rachel calmly unpacked two jars of baby food and a bottle of formula.

Hayley blinked back tears, her gaze darting to the window. Bright May sunshine bathed her parents' yard in a golden glow. There wasn't a cloud in the sky.

Empathy filled Rachel's eyes. "He'll come home."

"It's been four days, Rachel," Hayley whispered. "I haven't heard a word from Max. And now this. How do you know he'll come back to us?"

"I choose to believe and hope. We have a good, good heavenly Father, Hayley. He keeps His promises and loves Max."

"How do you know nothing bad has happened to him, though? It doesn't matter how good a climber he is, there are things outside of his control. Look what happened in Peru. We all thought he was gone forever."

"But God," Rachel said softly. "God gave Max a second chance. He didn't bring him home just to take him away again. God doesn't work like that."

Hayley exhaled, her tears threatening to spill over. "Wow. I had no idea your faith was so rock-solid. Thank you for reminding me of the truth."

Rachel smiled, sliding an arm around Hayley's shoulders. "And now, we're all going to pray and take good care of you."

Her family encircled her, their hands resting

on her shoulders, arms and head. Their earnest prayers cocooned her in warmth, offering hope and reinforcing the truth Rachel had shared. No matter what happened, God held them all in the palm of His hands—including Max.

"Please, please put this bird on the ground."

Max gripped the armrests tightly, his knuckles white as the helicopter rocked in the relentless wind. The whomp, whomp, whomp of the rotors stirred the snow into frenzied spirals, reducing visibility to nearly nothing as they approached the Fairbanks hospital's landing pad. Sweat trickled down his back despite the freezing temperatures. After three harrowing days stranded on Denali's unforgiving slopes, all he wanted was warmth, a hot drink, food—and Hayley.

The medic leaned over the injured climbers in their group, checking vitals and murmuring reassurances. Max hadn't been physically hurt, but his soul felt battered. The memories that had resurfaced on that mountainside had shaken him to his core. But despite the cold and exhaustion, God had watched over them. He knew that now.

Stranded in his tent, Max had come to understand so much about himself—about his mistakes, his fears and his failings. He'd already begged God for forgiveness. Now he needed to ask for Hayley's.

The helicopter tilted, the skids finding purchase

on the landing pad. Relief flooded Max as the medic raised a gloved hand to steady him.

"Easy, sir. Just a moment."

The doors opened, icy air whipping inside as the crew finished their safety checks. Finally, they signaled him forward. Max scrambled out, bracing against the wind, and stumbled across the pad, leaving his gear behind. He ducked into the hospital entrance, the sudden warmth enveloping him.

A nurse stepped forward, digital tablet in hand. "Sir, we need to examine you—"

"I'm fine," Max rasped. "I need to see my family."

The nurse hesitated but relented. "Down the corridor to your right. Double doors."

His boots squeaked on the linoleum as he jogged, his heart hammering. He turned the corner too quickly and found himself at a set of doors marked Do Not Enter.

"Wrong way, sir." Another nurse appeared, smiling. She tipped her head toward the opposite end of the corridor. "There's a pretty redhead waiting for you down there."

Hayley.

Max's chest tightened as he broke into a sprint, the adrenaline overriding his exhaustion. He pushed through the double doors into the waiting room.

Her gasp pierced the air, and in an instant, she was running toward him. Her auburn hair, loose and wavy, framed her tear-streaked face. She threw herself into his arms, and he caught her, burying his face in the crook of her neck.

"I'm sorry," he choked, his voice breaking. "I'm so sorry, Hayley."

She pulled back just enough to frame his face with her hands, her warm palms grounding him. Her green eyes glistened with tears.

"It doesn't matter," she whispered, her voice trembling. "Nothing else matters. You're alive. You're here."

Her face crumpled, and she started to cry. Max pressed his forehead against hers, his own tears falling freely. The noise of the waiting room faded as the world narrowed to just the two of them.

"Wait," he said hoarsely, glancing at the family members gathering around them. "I need a minute with Hayley, please."

They stepped back reluctantly, giving them as much space as the small room allowed. Max cupped Hayley's face, his thumbs brushing away her tears.

"Hayley, listen to me. I'm so sorry. Some of my memories came back while I was stuck in that tent, and I realized how much I've hurt you. I was so blind. So afraid. I used my family's issues as an excuse to push you away, but the truth is, loving you terrified me. You saw the real me, the parts I wanted to hide. And instead of embracing that,

I ran. Please forgive me. I'll never forgive myself if I've lost you."

She shook her head, her lips trembling. "Max, stop. I forgave you a long time ago. I love you. I've always loved you. And I've made mistakes, too. I put everyone else first because I was scared to admit I needed someone to take care of me. But you…you make me feel safe. You see me, Max. You've always seen me."

He leaned down, capturing her lips in a kiss that spoke of every apology, every promise and every ounce of love he carried for her. Cheers and whistles erupted around them, but Max didn't care. Hayley's arms wrapped around his neck, pulling him closer.

"All right, lovebirds," Wyatt teased, his grin wide. "Save some of that for later."

They broke apart, laughing softly. Max rested his forehead against Hayley's again, his hands firm on her waist.

"I love you," he said, his voice steady. "And I promise, I will never, ever take you for granted again. You'll always come first. Always."

"I love you, too," she whispered, her smile radiant through her tears. "And I believe you."

As he held her close, Max knew this wasn't just a reunion. It was a new beginning—the start of a life where love, faith and family would guide them through any storm.

Epilogue

One year later

Strands of vintage lights crisscrossing the Fairview Hotel's ballroom cast a warm glow over the intimate gathering, glinting off the party glasses and adding a festive flare to the evening. The delicious taco bar, adorned with fresh toppings, piles of tortilla chips and plenty of salsa was a hit with their guests. Couples filled the dance floor, enjoying the DJ's playlist mixed with upbeat pop songs and romantic ballads. But for Hayley, the most perfect part of the reception was the man sitting beside her—her husband.

Max leaned in, brushing her lips with his own, his smile radiating the kind of joy she'd never imagined she'd be blessed enough to share.

"Have I told you that you're a stunning bride?"

She grinned and kissed him back, her heart swelling with happiness. "Tell me again, please."

"You look gorgeous, Hayley. I'm so glad you agreed to marry me."

Her laughter bubbled up. "I'm so glad you limped back into my life, Max Butler. I'm a better woman because I get to be your wife."

His pale blue eyes locked on to hers, full of love and promise, and for a moment, it was as though the rest of the world faded away. She could have stayed in this moment forever, but a subtle glance at the wedding coordinator checking the time reminded her they had a cake to cut.

Just as she was about to stand, a gentle clinking of glass echoed through the room, silencing the hum of conversation.

"Uh-oh," Max murmured, a mixture of amusement and apprehension in his tone as they both turned toward the microphone.

Jack, Max's dad, stood there, his posture a bit awkward but his expression resolute.

"What's he doing?" Max asked, his brow furrowed. "Was this part of your plan?"

"No," Hayley whispered back, squeezing his hand. "Let's give him a chance."

Jack cleared his throat and offered a sheepish smile. "I know this isn't part of the wedding reception protocol," he began, his voice steady despite the tremor of emotion beneath it. He turned to smile at Max and Hayley, his gaze softening. "I hope the new couple will extend grace as I take a minute to say some things publicly that should have been said a long time ago."

Hayley felt Max stiffen beside her, and she silently prayed, *Lord, use this for good.*

Jack took a deep breath. "It's no secret that I've made mistakes—choices that hurt a lot of people, especially my family. And I've carried the weight of those mistakes for a long time. But tonight isn't about my shortcomings. It's about celebrating something extraordinary—love. The kind of love that heals, that forgives and that gives second chances."

A ripple of emotion spread through the room. Hayley blinked back tears as Jack's voice cracked.

"When we thought we'd lost Max," he continued, clearing his throat, "it was as though the light went out of our lives. And when God, in His infinite grace, brought him back to us, it was incredible—100 percent a second chance for all of us. Seeing the two of you together, the way you love each other so deeply and unselfishly, has been a gift beyond measure. Max and Hayley, I want you to know how proud I am of you both. Your love inspires me. It's taught me what it means to love sacrificially and unconditionally. And I have no doubt that there's no mountain you can't climb together."

By the time Jack stepped back from the microphone, there wasn't a dry eye in the room.

Hayley leaned her head against Max's shoulder, overcome. "Oh, my word," she whispered.

Max stood abruptly, pulling Hayley to her feet,

and they crossed the room. Jack's eyes filled with emotion as his son embraced him tightly.

"I love you, Dad," Max said, his voice thick.

"I love you too, son," Jack whispered.

When they pulled apart, Hayley hugged Jack too. Tonight they could finally let go of all of the old wounds.

The DJ started a new song, and the dance floor filled with their loved ones. Hayley caught sight of Fiona toddling toward her, looking adorable in her pink satin flower girl dress. With a laugh, she scooped the little girl up and spun her around.

The future stretched out before her, bright and full of possibility. Their engagement had been short—just under a year—but long enough to dream about this day and the life she and Max would build together.

After their honeymoon in the Bahamas, they would return to Opportunity, where their community awaited them. Their new indoor rec center, Stars Alley, was about to have its grand opening thanks to the timely grant from a national organization and generous contributions from local residents. They had big plans for its future—summer camps, recreational leagues and even more space for indoor sports. It was a shared dream, one that combined Max's love for adventure and her passion for helping people find a sense of belonging.

When Fiona squirmed to be let down, Hayley set her on her feet, and Max appeared beside her.

He took Hayley's hand, pulling her into his arms as a slow song began to play.

"I love you, Hayley," he murmured, his voice a soft rumble against her ear.

"I love you too, Max."

"Thank you for making me the happiest man alive," he said, kissing her deeply as their guests erupted into cheers and applause.

As they swayed together on the dance floor, Hayley closed her eyes, letting the moment sink in. Max had regained a significant amount of memories, but still struggled with occasional headaches. The neurologist had encouraged him to live his life without any restrictions. She didn't know what challenges the future might bring, but she knew this: together, they could face anything.

And with Max by her side, she was ready to climb every mountain, cross every river and weather every storm—because their love was worth it.

* * * * *

If you enjoyed this
Opportunity, Alaska, *book*
by Heidi McCahan,
be sure to pick up the first in the series,

Her Alaskan Family

Available now from Love Inspired.

Dear Reader,

I've always wanted to write a romance novel featuring a character with amnesia. Max Butler, a charming mountain climber from *Her Alaskan Family*, was the ideal man for the role. Little did I know an amnesia story is not all that easy to write. To be honest, I struggled with finishing this one. But God is always faithful to show up right when we need Him. This time was no exception, and I'm thrilled about how this one turned out.

Maybe you can relate. Maybe you've had big plans and thought everything would go smoothly until an obstacle landed in your path, and you weren't quite sure what to do. Much like Max and Hayley and all my fictional friends in Opportunity, Alaska, I often need a reminder of how God is with us in our struggles and our joyful experiences, and He loves second chances and redemption stories. As always, my hope is that reading this novel will inspire you to reflect on the truths found in God's word and strengthen your relationship with Him.

I hope you enjoyed your visit to Opportunity, and I look forward to sharing another story soon. Thank you for supporting inspirational fiction and telling your friends how much you enjoy our books. I'd love to connect with you. You can find me online: https://www.facebook.com/heidimccahan/, http://heidimccahan.com/ or https://www.instagram.com/heidimccahan.author. For news about book releases and sales, sign up for my author newsletter: http://www.subscribepage.com/heidimccahan-newoptin

Until next time,
Heidi

*What will it take to save her family's candy company...and end a decades-long feud?
Read on for an excerpt
from Heidi McCahan's full-length novel,*
A Winter of Sweet Secrets, *available now from Love Inspired Trade!*

The man drove like he'd never seen snow. At this rate, they wouldn't get to Evergreen until tomorrow. Jovi rattled the ice in her cup, left over from their dinner stop at a fast-food place, then took a long sip through her straw. She tried to discreetly lean across the center console to sneak a peek at the speedometer. They crept along at a lousy thirty-two miles per hour.

Stifling a sigh, she reached for the dial on the stereo and upped the volume on the radio. Some might say this song was overplayed, but she couldn't resist humming along to the iconic country hit.

Burke let go of the wheel just long enough to jab at the button and silence the music. "Do you mind? I'm trying to concentrate."

He resumed his white-knuckle grip and hunched farther over the steering wheel.

"You need total silence when you drive?"

"In treacherous conditions, yes."

"Got it." Jovi squirmed in the passenger seat. Sweat dampened the back of the white T-shirt she'd layered under her cardigan. Burke had the defroster cranked to its highest setting, and the heater pumping warm air into the vehicle. Rather than adjust any of the settings and risk aggravating him more than she already had, she'd have to peel off her outer layer.

She unclipped her seat belt and then shrugged off her jacket.

He glanced her way. The silvery light from the dash illuminated his pinched features. "What are you doing?"

She hesitated, her arm stuck in one sleeve. "Taking off my jacket. It's too hot in here."

"It's not wise to unbuckle while the vehicle's moving." Disapproval clung to every word. "Especially in these conditions."

Oh, dear. He really needed to simmer down a notch. Sure it had been snowing since they'd left Anchorage, but at least the wind wasn't blowing hard. They were totally safe. Ditching her jacket on the floorboard, she pulled her seat belt back on and quickly snapped it into place. "See? I'm safe as can be. Now I won't pass out. Which means I can keep you awake. So really, that was all for your benefit."

His one-syllable grunt made her smile. "Quick question. Have you ever driven in snow before?"

"Not recently. What was your first clue?"

"You're going under the speed limit, clutching that steering wheel like it's our lifeline, and, well, you look terrified. How'd I do? Are my observations accurate?"

"If I may, I'd like to point out that if we hadn't detoured to pick up your precious part, then we'd likely be much closer to our destination by now."

Her scalp prickled. Could he be any more obnoxious?

"Look, I get that you're annoyed I asked you to drive a measly four blocks out of your way to meet a lady who stayed after hours to make sure she handed that package to me in person. By the way, thanks to her willingness to go above and beyond the call of duty, I now have that *precious part* in my possession. And if we ever get to Evergreen, I'll be able to give it to my sister. Then hopefully, the mechanic will be able to install it, and a small family-owned company that provides several jobs for residents will be up and running smoothly again. So I apologize for the inconvenience, but on behalf of the many customers worldwide who enjoy their sweet treats from Evergreen Candy Company, thank you for understanding."

Whoa. She slumped back against the headrest, slightly out of breath.

Silence hung heavy between them.

Then the corners of his mouth twitched. "Feel good to get that all out?"

Ignoring his snide comment, she took another sip of her diet soda. The carbonated liquid slid down her throat. Maybe she should apologize.

That was kind of a lot. Yet she felt lighter somehow. Besides, somebody needed to tell him what was up, because he was kind of grinchy.

Good deeds and generosity didn't really seem like they were his thing.

Bright lights from a truck driving behind them illuminated the interior of their car. Burke held up his hand to shield his eyes from the reflection in the mirror. The other driver passed quickly. A spray of snow kicked up from the truck's tires and coated their windshield.

Grumbling under his breath, Burke twisted the knob and forced the windshield wipers to work at top speed. The truck's taillights glowed red, then disappeared into the darkness up ahead.

Jovi deposited her drink back in the cup holder. "Has anyone ever told you that you're grumpy?"

"Has anyone ever told you that you're sarcastic?"

"Just you." She studied his strong profile, noting the tension settling in his angular jaw. "Let me guess. You're not a fan?"

"It's a challenging communication style and one I find difficult to engage with."

"Oh, that's good to know. Thank you. Perhaps I'll try a kinder, gentler approach. Burke, you must be exhausted after traveling all day with a young child. What can I do to make this final leg of your journey more enjoyable?"

"See? That right there." Burke shot her another

exasperated look. "You didn't mean a word of that, did you?"

"Don't be ridiculous. I meant all of it. That was empathy."

"With a generous dose of sarcasm. Again, it's all in the tone."

She blew out a gusty breath. "You sure know how to make a hundred miles feel like a thousand."

"Happy to be of service."

They rode for a few more minutes in a terse silence until Burke cleared his throat. "Does it always snow like this here?"

Laughter bubbled from her lips. He shot her another look. This one fierce. She clamped her hand over her mouth. Darby Jane had fallen asleep about an hour ago. She didn't blame him for being upset if her outburst woke the sleeping child.

"Sorry," she whispered. "But you did just move to Alaska, right? Did no one tell you about the weather?"

"This seems a bit excessive."

She peered into the darkness. Their headlights tunneled into the road ahead, where the snow was now pelting them at a dizzying rate. An ominous feeling danced down her spine. Maybe he had a valid point. Now that she'd taken a closer look, this did seem like a lot of snow all at once.

"We've been on the road for almost three hours," Burke said. "Does it typically take this long to drive from Anchorage to Evergreen?"

"No, it shouldn't. This is only my second trip on this road, though. They finished building it about a year and a half ago."

"Before that people came and went from Evergreen by airplane?"

"Or dog sleds and snow machines. But yes, we relied mostly on planes."

"Wow." He shook his head in disbelief. "I can't imagine traveling anywhere by a team of dogs pulling a sled."

"It's not for everyone," Jovi said. "How did you decide you wanted to move to Evergreen if you're unaccustomed to snow?"

"My aunt has a place there. We visited several times when I was a kid, and those are some of my happiest memories. I wanted Darby Jane to experience an Alaskan winter."

"Who's your aunt?"

"Lois Phillips."

Jovi's breath hitched. "No way. Really?"

"Do you know her?"

Oh, wow. Where to begin? "Well, from what little I've been told, your aunt and my grandmother used to be the best of friends. Until they weren't. The Wrights and the Phillipses have been feuding for longer than you and I have been alive."

Burke drummed his thumb against the steering wheel. "So you're one of Carol and Dennis's granddaughters?"

"Yep. My sister, Isabel, is two years older." Jovi

angled her body more toward his. "Forgive me for asking, but did you and I meet when we were kids?"

He shook his head. "Aunt Lois didn't want me to play with Carol's grandkids. Ever. She made that quite clear. To be honest, she had so many activities planned when I visited, there wasn't time to wonder about the kids who lived nearby."

"I still can't believe they live down the road from one another and manage to never speak. Or they used to, anyway." Jovi softened her tone. "I was sorry to hear that Lois had passed."

"Thank you," Burke said. "I hate that Darby Jane didn't get to meet her or my uncle Mac. My mother, Lois's sister, well, they weren't exactly close. Polar opposites, really, and there's a substantial age difference. But I loved to visit Aunt Lois and Uncle Mac."

"They were good people," Jovi said. "Mac and Lois both loved Evergreen and always supported the community. I wish I knew why she and Grammie had a falling-out."

"Yeah, she and my uncle lived in several places throughout the years. He was in the military, and they moved quite a bit. But they seemed happiest in Evergreen."

"Agreed."

He looked over at her again.

"What?" She squirmed in her seat, surprised

by the way one side of his mouth lifted in a hint of a smile.

"We agreed on something."

"That your aunt and uncle were good people? That wasn't hard." She twisted the beaded bracelet on her wrist around in a slow circle. "Here's something we probably won't agree on."

"Oh?"

"Why don't you let me drive the rest of the way?"

"Absolutely not."

"Why not?"

"Because I've got this," he insisted. "And your name's not on the rental contract."

"You're a rule-follower, aren't you?"

"One hundred percent."

Don't miss this sweet Alaska-set story from Heidi McCahan!

Get up to 4 Free Books!

We'll send you 2 free books from each series you try PLUS a free Mystery Gift.

FREE Value Over $25

Both the **Love Inspired®** and **Love Inspired® Suspense** series feature compelling novels filled with inspirational romance, faith, forgiveness and hope.

YES! Please send me 2 FREE novels from the Love Inspired or Love Inspired Suspense series and my FREE gift (gift is worth about $10 retail). After receiving them, if I don't wish to receive any more books, I can return the shipping statement marked "cancel." If I don't cancel, I will receive 6 brand-new Love Inspired Larger-Print books or Love Inspired Suspense Larger-Print books every month and be billed just $7.19 each in the U.S. or $7.99 each in Canada. That is a savings of 20% off the cover price. It's quite a bargain! Shipping and handling is just 50¢ per book in the U.S. and $1.25 per book in Canada.* I understand that accepting the 2 free books and gift places me under no obligation to buy anything. I can always return a shipment and cancel at any time by calling the number below. The free books and gift are mine to keep no matter what I decide.

Choose one:
- ☐ **Love Inspired Larger-Print** (122/322 BPA G36Y)
- ☐ **Love Inspired Suspense Larger-Print** (107/307 BPA G36Y)
- ☐ **Or Try Both!** (122/322 & 107/307 BPA G36Z)

Name (please print)

Address   Apt. #

City   State/Province   Zip/Postal Code

Email: Please check this box ☐ if you would like to receive newsletters and promotional emails from Harlequin Enterprises ULC and its affiliates. You can unsubscribe anytime.

Mail to the Harlequin Reader Service:
IN U.S.A.: P.O. Box 1341, Buffalo, NY 14240-8531
IN CANADA: P.O. Box 603, Fort Erie, Ontario L2A 5X3

Want to explore our other series or interested in ebooks? Visit www.ReaderService.com or call 1-800-873-8635.

---

*Terms and prices subject to change without notice. Prices do not include sales taxes, which will be charged (if applicable) based on your state or country of residence. Canadian residents will be charged applicable taxes. Offer not valid in Quebec. This offer is limited to one order per household. Books received may not be as shown. Not valid for current subscribers to the Love Inspired or Love Inspired Suspense series. All orders subject to approval. Credit or debit balances in a customer's account(s) may be offset by any other outstanding balance owed by or to the customer. Please allow 4 to 6 weeks for delivery. Offer available while quantities last.

Your Privacy—Your information is being collected by Harlequin Enterprises ULC, operating as Harlequin Reader Service. For a complete summary of the information we collect, how we use this information and to whom it is disclosed, please visit our privacy notice located at https://corporate.harlequin.com/privacy-notice. Notice to California Residents – Under California law, you have specific rights to control and access your data. For more information on these rights and how to exercise them, visit https://corporate.harlequin.com/california-privacy. For additional information for residents of other U.S. states that provide their residents with certain rights with respect to personal data, visit https://corporate.harlequin.com/other-state-residents-privacy-rights/.

LIRLIS25